GENERATIONS

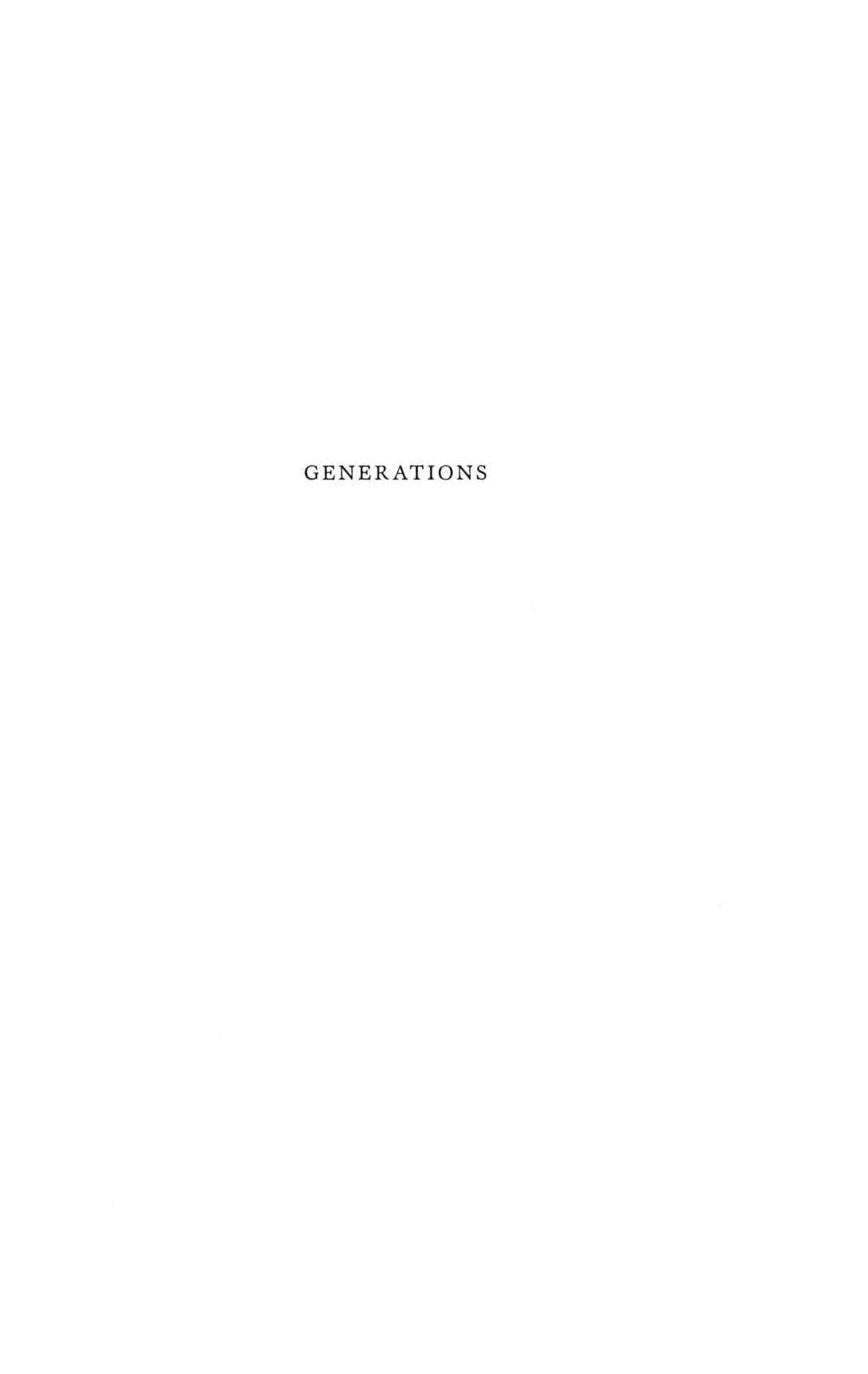

Generations
(stories)

George Strange

MERCER UNIVERSITY PRESS
2002

ISBN 0-86554-791-2
MUP/H598

© George Strange, 2002
Published by Mercer University Press
6316 Peake Road
Macon, Georgia 31210-3960
All rights reserved

First Edition.

This is a work of fiction. While, as in all fiction, the literary perceptions and insights are based on experience, all names, characters, places, and incidents are either products of the author's imagination or are used fictitiously. No reference to any real person is intended or should be inferred.

The paper used in this publication meets the minimum requirements of American National Standard for Information Sciences—Permanence of Paper for Printed Library Materials, ANSI Z39.48-1984.

Strange, George
  Generations : stories / by George Strange.—1st ed.
       p. cm.
  ISBN 0-86554-791-2 (hardcover : alk. paper)
 1. Southern States—Social life and customs—Fiction. I. Title.
  PS3619.T74 G46 2002
  813'.6—dc21
                                                    2002002664

Contents

Connecting Generations	9
River Caul	21
Mrs. Dickens Goes to the Drugstore	41
A Promise for George Washington Gonzales	55
Dust	61
Mockingbird	63
If She Should Die	89
Fireflies	113
Pears	125
Season of Death	145

This book, for generations future, present and past, is dedicated with love and gratitude to my sons, Jason and Josh, to my mother, Lou, to Alison and her generous, creative spirit, and to the memories of two gentle men: George Orley Strange, my father, a dandy, a wit, a loving man who during the last years of his life wore his suffering as easily as some people wear clothes; and Carter Wesley Chasteen, my step-grandfather, who never gave me anger, disdain, censure, or advice, but gave me instead, and always, love.

Acknowledgments

Special thanks to the Hambidge Center and to the Georgia Council for the Arts for supporting this collection of stories, to Mercer University Press's Marc Jolley, who kept the possibility alive, and Kevin Manus, who, with vision and detail, edits so superbly, and to journals that first published seven of the stories: APPALACHIAN HERITAGE—"Fireflies," *descant* —"If She Should Die," HABERSHAM REVIEW—"Pears," "Connecting Generations," KUDZU—"Mrs. Dickens Goes to the Drugstore," LULLWATER REVIEW—"Season of Death," THE FLORIDA TIMES UNION—"A Promise for George Washington Gonzales"

Connecting Generations

He was my grandfather and your great-grandfather. He told this story about his daddy. He told it at family reunions each June, starting when he was seventy-six. He told it for fifteen years, and then a few days after his ninety-first birthday he died. That first year I copied down part of the story and recorded a little more each year until I knew it by heart. The last two years he told it, I could match him word for word, pause for pause. He would start telling it on the porch. That's where he was when things started to change. Next he'd walk to the barn, then follow those two ruts through the pasture until he was out on the red clay road. All of us following along, listening to his telling. He'd stand in the road and point his finger toward the mountain and the apple orchard beyond, and we could hear the blasts from the horses' nostrils that long-ago night, could see the black trunk bounding about on the wagon bed with Jake bent over at the reins, the solitary lantern glowing like a large firefly, and your great-grandfather desperately hurling his father's name through cupped hands. The telling always ended in the bedroom he'd stayed in as a child. Once again, he'd be pointing, his finger leading our eyes to the quilt, and his voice so soft and sincere I could see the little boy he had been, sweating and huddled with fright. He had a reason for wanting us all to hear this story each year. You keep

Generations

hearing it from me, and you'll know it by heart yourself one day. It's a way of connecting generations.

It was not the first time he had heard the story, but the first time, as his mother said, it had "struck him," this story of an ancestor who long ago had killed a man. Leaning against the front seat to hear his mother's telling more clearly, he dismissed the aromas of fried chicken, biscuits, and peach cobbler as they rose from the family's best serving dishes and permeated the bamboo picnic basket. A man dying in an apple orchard on a summer day, dying because the boy's great-great-grandfather had aimed a pistol and pulled the trigger. The story had such an effect on the boy that he fell backwards and drew in his breath quickly. Maybe they were all killers then. Him, his mother, all who would gather at the farm once more on this third Sunday in June. He drew his breath deeply and tried to imagine the man with red in his mustache and death in the curve of his finger.

The story was told before they had been gone an hour, before they had even reached McRae. Because there were five hours left of their drive from Dogwood to the reunion in the mountains, the boy's mother was thinking which traveling game—sign, car, or animal—they would play so the boy's father could concentrate on climbing the long trunk of Highway 441.

The boy didn't need her help. He had started his own game. He called it Find Great-Great-Grandfather Roberts. His first prospect was a red-headed man driving a cart on the Little Ocmulgee Golf Course, but the man was fat and had no mustache. He knew Mister Roberts had to be lean. He peered at the faces in oncoming cars and looked for him among the old men tending their roadside gardens and among the pedestrians on the sidewalks of Dublin.

Before they got to Athens, two things made him laugh. Neither had anything to do with Mister Roberts. The first was the house near the kaolin plant in McIntyre. The house had three wooden butterflies attached to a wooden shutter. One butterfly was half as large as the shutter. Above his spread wings were a momma butterfly and a baby butterfly. Passing Lake Sinclair, he laughed at swimmers being watered top and bottom as a quick, heavy rain emptied into the lake—cold, wet darts zinging into the heads of swimmers. The heads floated on the water like fishing bobbers with faces. Farther along he saw a red-bearded man using vigorous paddling strokes to push his canoe to a boat house. *That's what Mister Roberts would be in*, the boy thought. *He probably doesn't know much about motors. Also, he would be looking for a safe place. That's why he had left in the black trunk, bouncing like a hailstone on the back of a wagon.*

–Is that him? the boy asked, urgently pointing. Mister Roberts, there?

The car had passed the cove, and, looking back, his mother saw nothing but trees.

–No. Mister Roberts has been dead a long time.

–I bet he's not. I bet he got to Atlanta.

–Perhaps, his father said. But he was forty then, so he'd be one hundred and thirty now. We don't live that long in this country. Of course he might have gone to Tibet or found that mountain range in Russia where people live so long.

–If he did, the boy said excitedly, he might be coming home today.

–Your daddy's teasing you. He didn't go to those places.

–I don't see what's so funny about dying, the boy said and stuck his tongue out at his father.

In Athens his father won back his heart by taking him to a corner shop and buying him a two-dollar chocolate apple, which could not be eaten until after the family reunion dinner, and by buying from a nearby shop an on-the-spot consumable, a two-scoop mint chocolate chip ice cream in a waffle cone. His mother wiped his face with a napkin as they were leaving the shop.

Generations

Looking up at his mother, he knew how Mister Roberts's son had felt holding up the apple-buttered mouth to Granny Zell's dress.

After they crossed a busy street and were almost to the tall trees and rich, green grass, his parents made him pose on the top step near a black arch. His mother told him that one day he'd walk under that arch just as they had done. Yet they stopped him when he started through so he'd be done with that challenge.

–Don't rush it, his mother said. It's soon enough you'll be a college senior.

–I don't even know what Mister Roberts looks like, the boy said. Can I see his picture when we get there?

–I imagine Aunt Eve started a fire with that thing long ago, his mother laughed.

–Did you ever see it?

–I saw it when I was little girl. It hung over the mantel until Granny Zell died. Aunt Eve had it down before the funeral.

–Why did she do that?

–She hated him for what he had done.

–Without him, we wouldn't be here. He's a part of us.

–A missing part, his mother said quickly. That's the way he chose, and that's the way it is.

–I'm going to find him, the boy said confidently.

–What's there to find? his father asked. Never was much to him in the first place, so I hear. Just a drifter, a bit of scum lodged for a while in a log jam on the river.

–You wouldn't have us if he hadn't come this way. Momma. Me. We wouldn't *be* without him.

–What do you say to that? she asked her husband.

–Pass me a biscuit.

–Well, I like that, she said.

They drove through Commerce and Cornelia. Blue mountains lay quietly to the north. His father had told him once that giants all wore blue pants. Like children stretching out on fishing piers and hanging their heads toward the water, the giants sprawled, their huge butts sticking up in the air, as they hung their heads off the edge of the world and looked deep into space.

There were other landmarks in this region of giants. Apples, the size of marbles but green and growing, dangled from the leafy crowns of orchards. Wooden shacks, open on three sides, displayed peaches, Vidalia onions, jellies, and syrups. Large, black cast-iron kettles, sitting on scraps of lumber, awaited the harvest of peanuts.

On their drive, the boy watched the earth change from white sand to red clay. Soon the boy's father would turn the car away from 441's broad trunk and would follow the meandering limbs of county roads as they shot northward through Georgia.

–Tell me, tell me again, the boy insisted, about how he came into this county when there was almost no one here, how he drove up in his wagon with the two black trunks and how after he killed the man he escaped by hiding in one of the trunks and being driven to the train station.

–That's about it, she said. You know it all.

And then they were driving through the pasture. The farmhouse sat on a rise to the left. They stopped to let cattle pass.

–See that bull there, his father pointed. That drooling, senseless animal. Some men are fathers, some are bulls. Mister Roberts was a bull. He wandered in, got what he wanted, wreaked havoc and ran away. Don't concern yourself with him. I don't know what Granny Zell saw in an animal like that.

–She loved him, though, the boy's mother spoke softly. Said she always did.

–Come on, the boy said. Tell me one more time. And tell me what's in that black trunk in the basement.

–Nothing but Mister Roberts's skeleton, his mother said and laughed.

Generations

    –I'm going to find him, the boy said without smiling. You just wait and see. And I won't play with my boring cousins.
    –Why does old Aunt Eve hate her daddy so? the boy asked, running up to his parents huddled among kin. It happened almost a hundred years ago. Aren't we supposed to forgive people after seventy or eighty years?
    –She was about your age when it happened. Imagine how you would feel if your daddy killed a man, then ran off and you never saw him again. No daddy to buy you chocolate apples and mint chocolate chip ice creams. What would you think of such a man? She brushed at his hands. Where did you get so dirty?
    In the basement, that's where, but he wouldn't tell her. He planned to go back; he knew he'd find the answer there.
    –He killed a man. Does that mean we're all killers?
    –Of course not, his mother laughed. The others laughed, too. The bald, the fat, the lame, all laughed. I'm the daughter of a man. Does that make me a man?
    –We're all children of God, aren't we?
    –Yes, she said.
    –So that makes us like God.
    –Not enough like.
    –But like God.
    –Yes.
    –Then if we all came from a killer, we have to be like him.
    –You're being ridiculous, she said. Leave us alone and grab a plate before all the food is gone.

    The boy stood in the middle of one of the pulsating lines beside a long series of tables made of sawhorses and plywood tops, set up in a bowl-like valley below the farmhouse. Portatoilets had been placed in a hickory grove to cut down the traffic in and out of Aunt Eve's house. Aunt Eve is pushing a hundred, the boy's mother had told him, and doesn't need the shock of all these people in her house.

Hearing the conversations all about him, he knew he must be part of a dying family. Talk of divorce, disease, and death squeezed his appetite and changed the appearance of food. The once soft-looking dumplings became greasy in their attachment to congealed chicken. There were green beans laced with hog fat, creamed corn of a sickening consistency, casseroles steaming like baked compost.

–Eve, whose boy is that over there with the dirty hands?

In answer, the old lady pointed to the boy's mother.

–Can't be. She was always so neat. Cried if she got dirt on her hands, remember? I bet she doesn't know he's standing in line with filth all over him. Kids got no respect anymore.

Watching plates bend under the weight of generous helpings, he lost his appetite completely. The feast of killers made him queasy. Maybe a sip of something would make him feel better. Snaking a hand through others, he touched a cup, but a hand arrested his and started tugging him away.

–Boy, Aunt Eve said, that's disgraceful. Reaching over food with dirty hands. Bet you were taught better than that.

–Let me go, he pleaded. He could feel her body straining against his pull.

–I'll let you go when your hands are decent.

He saw hate in her eyes. *This one is a killer for sure*, he thought. *She's got a big helping of the killer's blood.*

–You're his daughter, aren't you?

–What are you talking about?

He tried to tear away from her.

–Boy, she said, pulling him out of the line as relatives laughed loudly. I'm old, but I can still handle you.

His mother went along, too. They made him wash his hands, but they couldn't make him go back. He'd rip the tables apart if

Generations

they took him back, and his mother and Aunt Eve knew he would. Besides, he knew that the time the others spent stuffing themselves was the perfect time to slip into the basement.

–Don't you go back down there, Aunt Eve warned. It's no place for a child to be. It's dirty. Got no telling how many poisonous spiders. Got our orchard sprays. You keep out of there.

Aunt Eve waited for his reply.

–You will do as Aunt Eve asks, won't you?

He nodded his head, then watched his mother and the old lady walk toward the lines of people, moving like two fat centipedes beside the tables.

A moment later he opened the basement door to the smell of rotten apples. Halfway down the unpainted wooden stairs he saw the remains of last year's harvest floating in their own brown juice. On shelves above the puddles were old hammers, screwdrivers, nails, jars, and dust-coated plastic and glass gallon jugs. He wrote his name on one of the glass jugs, then cleared out the center of the O. Through the circle he saw murky, brownish-gold fluid sitting in dumb, dull wait. He realized how thirsty he was as he stood in the one patch of sunlight that came through the one small window. The window was like a picture frame. Gathered in its borders were a distant, blue mountain and a piece of sky.

Thirst could wait. He had to get back to the large black chest with brass latches, lock, and binding. The chest reminded him of stories of pirates and plunder, forbidden treasures of the past. For the boy, the smell of apple was a mixture of danger and pleasure.

Because he had been told so many lies—he hoped—about what was inside, he was hesitant to pry the lid up too quickly. He tapped lightly.

He couldn't remember who had said what because the suggestions had been so vivid to his mind that the speakers hung in the air like the aroma of apples, invisible but present, while the answers materialized, hardened, and glowed before his eyes: Apple seeds... skeletons... switches for mean little children... another black trunk... gold... cats' tongues... Mister Roberts... old clothes... a tunnel to China... midnight... spiders... a cider press... diamonds... snakes....

Not wanting to invite either joy or desolation without deliberation, he stood over the chest for several minutes before raising the lid, which was lighter than he thought it would be. The mustiness was so tangible it was almost overpowering. He quickly dropped the lid.

He needed fortification. Perhaps a drink like the cowboys downed in the old Western movies his father liked to watch. A shot of alcohol to fortify themselves for what lay ahead.

Clouds blocked the sun, making the basement even darker. What if something reached out and pulled him down into the trunk? His daddy told him once that was how the devil got cub scouts for his den. He found little boys doing things they shouldn't be doing, things they were hiding from God. And when the devil found such a boy he was on him faster than a grasshopper and dragging him face first through the earth, before the boy even had time to cry out.

It was dark, and he was where he had been told not to be. He was sweating as he touched the trunk.

—I've got to be fortified first, he said, patting the lid of the trunk.

He went back to the jar he had left the O on and unscrewed the lid.

The fortifying stuff burned his lips and inside his mouth. It stung his throat and stomach, too. The stuff tasted awful. It did

Generations

in the movies, too. The one who had been fortified often chased his drink with a wince and a gasp.

Once fortified, there was no turning back.

—There are some things in life that have to be done alone. This is one of them.

He wasn't conscious of gaining courage from the drink or from the pronouncement, yet soon after one was swallowed and the other uttered he was opening the trunk, looking for Mister Roberts.

As he lifted the lid, his shoulders slumped.

—Nothing but air, he sighed and then stopped.

He bent over and looked more closely. What he had thought was the bottom, wasn't. It was Mister Roberts.

He rested upside down on the trunk's cedar bottom. The boy removed the large picture frame and took it to the steps beneath the window.

A distinguished, rounded face capped with wavy hair. The eyes were big, the eyebrows light and the mustache red and prominent, covering from upper lip to nose and running to mid cheek. The eyes seemed, to the boy, to indicate a kind and protective personality. The chin was dimpled, just like the boy's. There was a handsomeness and a sly courage in the man's face that made the boy proud they were kin.

You don't look like a bull to me, the boy said. Do you know what I mean? He touched Mister Roberts's nose affectionately through the dust.

—Here, he said, holding out a bottle to him. Bet you're even thirstier than I am. You'll need a lot of fortification before you face that crowd out there. You don't know, Mister Roberts, what your family has come to. Before I got here today, your daughter Eve was pushing one hundred. A little while ago she got me. That makes one hundred and one. She'll push you, too, if you don't watch out. She's really got it in for you.

The boy tilted the bottle and liquid streaked down the glass in the frame. The boy stared at the moisture that appeared to be flowing through the mustache.

The boy tilted the bottle and drank heavily, his eyes squinting against the taste.

—Come on now, he said, gripping the frame firmly. You haven't seen these people in a long time. I hope you won't be disappointed with us.

In the apple orchard above the noisy clatter of people passing a year's news, the boy and his great-great-grandfather leaned against two tree trunks and looked down at their other relatives.

—I'm not sure, the boy said, but I think Granny Zell is really lonely after these years of looking down from the mantel all by herself. And talk about looking. Your son spent his life looking for you. About every firefly he ever saw, he wondered was it Jake coming back with you, the wagon, and the lantern. Isn't there somehow you can get in touch with him and ease his concern a bit? And finally, there's your daughter Eve. I know she's not happy. She's so bossy and mean. I think she might be catching the menopause. He glanced at Mister Roberts to see if the man acknowledged the boy's skill with language. Maybe this is none of my business but seemed like someone needed to have a talk with you. And I've just got to know why you killed that man. What's it like to kill somebody? To die? Nobody's ever told me.

His companion remained silent and stared dead ahead.

He tried, but there was no way he could lift Mister Roberts above the mantel to the high position next to Granny Zell, who waited, her hair pulled tightly across her scalp so it seemed she had no more hair than did her husband. Her eyes, smaller and

Generations

keener than those of Mister Roberts, stared at the two males in the room.

The boy drove the nail in the wall. He had chosen a spot halfway between the fireplace and the door. The nail's pressure forced lightning-like cracks between nail and mantel, nail and floor.

His stomach felt like nails were being driven clear through. He was very tired as he lifted Mister Roberts onto the nail. Sitting on the floor, he looked at his work. The pictures were angled so Granny Zell could step down to the mantel, then to her husband, or her husband could use the mantel and climb to her. The cracks in the wall looked like fragile strings connecting the two walled faces.

As night approached, some of the gathering moved toward the house. Eve and the boy's mother were in that group. As though head of the procession, a firefly bearing a golden torch flew into the house. The boy didn't see it. He was still on the floor in the room with his great-great-grandparents.

River Caul

Most people call the multi-windowed room next to the delivery room a nursery, but we river people might as well call it the aquarium. When one of us is brought blanketed into that room, we, the watchers in the hallway, motion for the nurse to take away the blanket. We want a thorough look: Is the chest broad enough to grow lungs that will be strong underwater, are the fingers long, do the hands and feet have the curves of boat paddles? We can sense a baby's buoyancy in the arms of a nurse. You know how in a swimming class the instructor will put one hand under the head of a student, another under the back of the knees. The student who will be able to float lies easy and unafraid in the instructor's hands, unconcerned about the moment when those helping hands will be withdrawn. The student who will never learn to float, or will learn only after great effort, struggles in the instructor's hands. The student's head rises in alarm and must be coaxed back to the instructor's waiting hand. Do you know, also, that a baby who will be a good swimmer is already exercising in the nursery, throwing arms about to build muscle, plying those long fins in steady arc as though already acquainted with the river that will be its home?

Gathered in the hallway outside the aquarium we watch the first strokes of our little swimmers. When Diamond Jim was brought in, his hands never struck air; he kept them close to the

Generations

bosom of the nurse. He flailed them about only when the nurse was putting him in his crib; then he swept the air like the frightened float student grabbing for something to hold on to. Once he was in his crib, he put those tested baby hands to his chest and left them there. On the other side of the window, we moved our arms in the motion of swimmers. We stood there a long time that first night of Diamond Jim's life, showing him how to stroke air, for we knew that if he were ever to be happy among us, he must develop arms that—like fins—fan easy, strong, and free in water.

By the time we are two or three years old, many of us have already developed swimming strokes and an affinity for water. When he was two years old, Diamond Jim's parents bought him a wading pool, yellow surfaced, populated by smiling blue dolphins. Unable to entice him by themselves, they filled the pool with warm water and invited the community kids. Our kids, some of them in diapers, ran laughing through that wading pool. They fell in, sucked up great mouthfuls, spit them out on each other, and splashed so hard that the leaves on the dogwood tree beside the pool dripped. Our kids were drawn to the water, all, so that at one time twenty attached themselves to that pool. The tiny area so crowded that some could claim only a submerged hand, or a foot atop another's wet elbow, but they were a mass in water, like a mess of fish in a live well. Diamond Jim dripped, too, but far from the others. He gripped the porch railing with both hands, his plump, pale body dimpled in sunlight. His only wetness, fright, soaked through his diapers and puddled upon the bricks. The other kids loved our element water, felt secure in it, saintly and blessed as though the yellow wading pool was the baptismal font of God. Those other kids, wet, holy, and full of power, taunted Diamond Jim, pointing toward the wetness dripping from his diaper as though pointing out the sin, dark but fathomable, of a two-year-old child.

Although Diamond Jim's parents made the other kids leave, they left the water in the wading pool.

For months, Diamond Jim didn't go near the pool. Rain, leaves, and time assaulted the yellow sides until they mildewed; the dolphins' smiles hid beneath fungus, as though the mammals swam circles in a stagnant sea. Inside the pool, the water turned as dark as Diamond Jim's favorite drink: Coke. The hypnotic power of that water, dark as our river, designed and organized our next attempt to get Diamond Jim into the pool.

Five of us helped Diamond Jim's parents scrub and disinfect the dolphins and the tiny inland sea. Then we each grabbed a bottle opener, a bottle, and started the rain of caps on the soft, green lawn. Diamond Jim stood off to the side, his round arms stretched toward us, his chubby face beaming at the Coke fog forming in the air about him.

—No, his father said. You can't have a bottle. You'll have to drink out of the pool.

We didn't have any two- and three-liter bottles like now. It took a truckload of the six-ounce bottles to fill the yellow pool. A mound of pale-green bottles glinted and grew in sunlight. Some landed bottoms up. Under the pecan trees, a roll call of America: Missoula, Montana; Little Rock, Arkansas; Duluth, Minnesota; Jacksonville, Florida. Every state in the union made a contribution, so we always felt the whole nation and not just our community coaxed Diamond Jim.

A brown foam spread across that tiny ocean. The air heavy with the sound of gurgling bottles, until at last the scrubbed mouths of the blue dolphins overflowed with effervescence. We had that wading pool so agitated that Coke bubbles leaped as high as our heads and splattered us. We adults, we fillers of pools, we instructors of swimmers, were laughing at the spectacle, while our would-be convert, Diamond Jim, diaper-laden, ran crying into the house.

Generations

After that disaster, we couldn't really blame his father for his next attempt: a trip to the beach. We knew the frustration he felt. Most of us barely distinguished river from ocean, so constantly we took to water by the time we were two and three years old, but there on the beach at St. Simons, arms folded over his forehead to shade his eyes from the sun, there like baby cowardice bronzed, Diamond Jim froze completely. Four years old, he stood on the beach, dry sand no less; he wouldn't even venture out onto the wet, hard-packed sand, glistening and inviting after the wash of ocean.

Small, foam-tipped waves rippled across the surface of the shore-bound Atlantic as the father grabbed his son's statue arm and dragged him toward the water. Diamond Jim screamed and pointed toward the waves.

—Why are there so many? he gasped.

Angry, his father wanted to tell him that the whitecaps were attached to the heads of the dead, all those who had ever died at sea: explorers, adventurers, pirates, sailors, passengers, little kids swept from knee-deep water by unrelenting undertow. All the water's dead from all the years, from the beginning of time, emerged, just barely surfacing so that all that could be seen of them were the silly white caps they wore. They and their caps bobbed and churned on the angry sea, while their submerged faces long dead and their eyes long dimmed looked once more landward, looked and remembered the land, the people they had left. Wanted to tell him in words a child could understand, but he refrained from such harshness and instead folded his arms across his chest and shouted: Get on back to the car. Least I won't have to watch you fail again. Cry there all you want, but don't let me see you crying by water ever again.

River Caul

Before he turned to go, Diamond Jim's big eyes looked into his father's mouth and saw whitecaps in the spittle on his father's tongue.

Diamond Jim's approaching adolescence called for more deliberate planning. That night there were three plotters inside: Diamond Jim's father, and the Doctors Kicklighter: Zandell, the medical doctor; Raven, his son, the vet. Diamond Jim waited out in the car. From there he could see one part of the cabin's interior: a shelf on the east wall.

Under the full moon, the tin roof shone as brightly as the river. A wooden deck, jutting over the river, was lit by its own moon, a solitary bulb suspended from a frayed electric wire. Fog swarmed over the roof and swooped toward the river, rushing the light like a vaporous moth.

Now years later the shack is still a one-room squatter beside the river. There is no bathroom. BATHE IN THE RIVER OR STINK admonishes the sign on the south wall. The east wall is laddered with shelves. On one shelf basks the bleached skull of an alligator, his mouth open; his large teeth, insecure but smug, curve inward. The visible teeth are all loosened and are easily removed. Beneath them a replacement set sits in dull wait. If someone handed you an alligator tooth, you probably couldn't identity it. You might think it a petrified finger. It has the curve of finger, the look of finger, wrinkled on top, swollen near the "fingernail;" the tip of a mature alligator tooth is the size of the hard, pointy fingernail of an old man or woman.

Years before, when Raven put a tooth into Diamond Jim's hand, the boy turned red. All OVER red, Raven told us. I bet if he had taken off his shoes, I'd seen a gaggle of red toes.

There was not much from the river that hadn't been forced into his hands. A gasping redbreast, green, yellow, and red, a

Generations

sparkling rainbow in sunlight; beaver walking sticks, tupelo limbs cut to size and stripped of bark by the river's flattails; baby softshelled turtles; artifacts living and dead placed in those trembling hands by his parents' and by our love, for we thought if he learned the river he would not fear it.

Diamond Jim sat insulated, comfortable in the car. With the windows rolled up he couldn't even hear the river, yet he knew all too well it was there. Waiting. For him. He knew that we wouldn't give up any more than the river would. A boy who is born into a river community like ours should at least pretend he has gills and fins. We all leap from the shore into the river as easily and naturally as rain falls from the sky. The river is in our blood; its song rocks our beds and opens our eyes to morning.

Even as the men planned, their eyelids felt heavy, their breathing slowed and grew smoother, for the river's quiet song runs deep within us. Inside the cabin, they planned and grew sleepy; outside, Diamond Jim waited in his father's car. They did not want him to hear, did not want to look at his big, frightened eyes.

From the car, the boy saw the men talking beneath the dirty, white skull of the jazzy-eyed alligator. Large hollows, which once held the eyes, added color to the room. One green bulb, one red, burned in the optic caverns, as the three men engaged in their own skullduggery.

—One day, the boy's father said, reaching into a tackle box, Diamond Jim was in the store and he kept glancing around, looking worried. Being afraid of water's one thing, I said. Don't tell me you're afraid of clothes hanging on racks, too? He told me they were creepy. That they looked like all the flesh had been dragged out of them and carted off somewhere by a strong river current. And you know what else he said?

Diamond Jim's father looked up from the tackle box: This is what he said, this shows how bright he is. He said: You hope my fear is learned and can be rectified; I know it is innate and fatal.

If you had walked out to the car and pointed your flashlight's beam into the back seat, you would have seen a frightened twelve-year-old boy, a prisoner just as surely as a man handcuffed in the back seat of a police cruiser. Diamond Jim wore wide, white tennis shoes, Huffy jeans, and a white t-shirt. The night was warm, a night that should have been free of sweat or shiver. Yet Diamond Jim's t-shirt was soaked with sweat; his rounded breasts and dark nipples showing like the bosom of a budding girl through the transparent shirt. So, too, was his smooth, pale face sweaty, his blonde hair stringy and stuck to his forehead as though he had only moments before walked dripping from the river he so dreaded. And his blue eyes so wide, so intelligent, yet not insightful or not courageous enough to find vistas other than water, for surely he must have known that a community that works, plays, swears, and loves by the river would make him of the river, even if the making killed.

They took out their cheapest, rustiest lures and placed them in a sacrificial tackle box, also cheap and rusty. When the boat overturned, they would not lose their clothes; the paddles would float and be recovered. But they would lose fishing rods and tackle box. What use disguise when the sham of fishermen sank?

–He's strong, Diamond Jim's father said. There must be some way he can use that strength against the river, instead of always worrying about how the river's going to use its strength against him. I'm telling you we can't just pick Diamond Jim up and throw him in the water; they'll hear the hissing all the way to town, and we'll spend a week digging fingernails out of our bodies. I'm telling you, this is the best way.

–And hernias out of our guts, Doctor Kicklighter added. He's a big boy.

Generations

—He's strong, I'm telling you. Strong in his fear. God what he could do if he'd learn to join that strength to courage.

—Daddy tells me he learned to swim that way, Raven said. His own daddy tossed him into the river.

—No, wasn't me learned that way. My daddy told me his daddy did him like that. Tell you the truth, in all my years on the river, I've never witnessed that teaching technique, that sudden, unexpected immersion.

Maybe it was simply legend, folklore, that when you find yourself in deep water, you find in the same instant buoyancy, courage, a swimming stroke. We had heard it happens, yet had never seen it. Diamond Jim was our guinea fish. We figured that come morning we would find a legend swimming in our river, or we would drag a waterlogged failure ashore and leave it to rot in the sand.

Sometime later, they coaxed Diamond Jim out of the car and onto the deck attached to the back of the shack. Upstream a bull gator bellowed. Beams from the deck light charged through the spaces between decking and cut into the water below, giving the river an artificial murkiness. The light swept across Diamond Jim. He had planted his tennis shoes firmly against the deck and leaned forward as though he feared the back of the bench not stout enough, feared that it would give to any pressure and send him backflipping into the river.

—I'm going to ask you flat out, Raven said. Why are you so afraid of water?

—You can't see that I'm afraid, can you?

—Godamighty, what do you think? You're leaning forward, like the river's trying to grab you.

—I'm always afraid somebody's going to push me in.

—Somebody needs to, the boy's father said, his disgust echoing with every footstep as he walked across the deck and into the shack.

River Caul

Raven stayed out in the night with the boy, for Raven knew, as we all do, that if you have fear you cannot claim the river; if you have fear, the river will claim you.

Diamond Jim was too young to know that unaltering patience and compliance, like other untreated diseases, can be deadly. Though the boy thought Raven's request crazy, Diamond Jim did as asked: he stretched out belly down on the deck and looked at the light cutting down into the water.

Diamond Jim was probably the best deck and poolside swimmer we have ever had. God knows how many hours of instruction he had been given. There on the deck he lifted his large legs and worked them with as smooth a flutter as you'd ever want to see; his legs adorned themselves with goose bumps just as though he were moving through cold water. And graceful he was, turning his head to the side every five strokes.

Raven kept him at it a long time with the night hovering about, the bridge standing stark watch, the river rolling past.

Later, as the boy brushed his teeth and we settled for the night in the cabin, Raven said excitedly: That boy is a by-God, certifiable, Olympic Dry Dock Gold Medalist.

There is something in parenthood that is of itself both noble and sinister, there is something unstated, unenforceable, yet accepted as law, something that requires the child surpass in some way, in looks, in wit, in cunning, in prowess, in achievement, in courage, the station of the father.

Later, Raven told some of us gathered along the shore that Diamond Jim reminded him of the lead steer in the cattle drives that were popular features of the western movies of Raven's youth. The lead steer reaching the river and wanting to turn back, yet finding its will no match for the determination of the herd, which pushes and pushes and pushes until the startled steer, driven into deep water, must either sink or swim.

Generations

There is nothing subtle or circular about a herd; it plunges forward as though blinded, as though the only passage were straight, deep, and narrow.

The river slipped past us as we waited in the dark of the cabin for morning. The pre-dawn gray carried light enough to illumine the lumps that were Diamond Jim and his father. They slept in the same bed. Both slept on their sides with their heads turned toward the bridge. Both had shoulders that curved downward under the cover. Diamond Jim's toes poked out from beneath the cover. His legs straight as though coaxing the skeleton within his body to grow more quickly to the length of that of his patterning father, whose legs were drawn up as though he slept in an overturned chair.

The river was a great band of fog when we pushed off from shore and headed upstream. Bound, Diamond Jim couldn't paddle. A cast iron weight hooked to a logging chain hung down to the links of the coiled chain that rested in the hull. The other end of the chain wrapped around the boy's neck, pulling his head down toward the gunwales, forcing his vision upon water, his enemy. The boy's feet pressed against the tackle box as the other three worked to find an efficient rhythm and position for the paddles.

The plotters weren't cruel. They hadn't looped the chain about the boy. There was no chain. Fear fixed him. He held onto the thwart with both hands. The men enjoyed the work of their muscles against the flow of river, enjoyed watching the fog itself to wisps before disappearing.

–What would you name that spot? his father asked, pointing to a clump of cypress roots at the river's edge.

–Don't know, Diamond Jim said.

—We call it the Choir Loft. See how it looks like tiers. Raven and I passed it one time, and it was filled with blackbirds wearing their dark robes.

—A choir of by-God singers from Hell, Raven added as he pointed to a bluff a quarter of a mile long on the other side of the river. What's that called?

Diamond Jim didn't want to name the marks along the river. His father's shoulders slumped. The river is yours if you name it.

A heavy roll of fat, like a puffy elastic band, secured the top of the boy's shorts to his midsection. His size and his inability to swim proof of Nature's duality. His flab, the spacing of molecules, should have given him buoyancy, a swimmer's friend. His fear of water punctured buoyancy.

Those of us in fishing shacks, in our riverside fields, or out in our boats saw the tableau, the four trapped for a moment in the river by the red net of the rising sun. Unmindful of weight limits, unrestricted by the net's mesh, we scurried aboard. The boat carried not four, but all.

We, who live by the river and are of the river, insist that Diamond Jim, who lives by the river, be of the river. We pull him toward deep water even though we know that there he will die. We know Diamond Jim would be happier if he knew how to swim, if he dove into the water and surfaced with a smile on the far side. We also know he can't do that, and that he would be content if we loosed our grip and let him return to shore. We can't. We are community; if he is of us, he must be like us. We can't let him think it would be all right if he never learned to swim. We can loosen our grip. We can let him hurry back to the safety of the cabin he so recently left. We can even say, That's all right, Jim. Say it if our eyes and our countenances say the opposite. We can hand him a towel, but we are the water he rubs from his body; we soak into his towel, and, when the towel dries, he may think we are gone.

Generations

    Listen, Diamond Jim. Are we gone? We are the river singing beneath the trees, we roll beneath the bridges you cross, we are the odor and sizzle of fish fries, the gleam of boats in tow along the roadways. We are never far from you.

    Within the past year a tiny island, no bigger than the bloated body of a drowning victim, had appeared. As we paddled by, we saw in the sand what we usually saw, a raccoon's footprints on Raccoon Island. But this morning, blood clotted in the footprints' and the grass was beaten down as though something large had passed through in the night.

    And so we passed along our river and its landmarks: Moccasin Bend, where, as a boy, Doctor Kicklighter saw a large water moccasin drop into the river from a tupelo tree; Beaver Palisades where the flattails have chewed the tops off trees and left their rooted stumps with sharp points like the walls of old wooden forts; Raincoat Junction, where a ripped, faded green plastic raincoat hung for years in tree limbs near where Shiler's Creek enters the river. Heading upstream along the throat of this watery kingdom that is our home, we sang joyfully the old songs and raised our paddles in salute to the old landmarks. Three of us did. Diamond Jim kept his eyes down toward the hull. His posture disgusted us, yet we knew we must be patient, we must bring the river to him.

    Our destination: a spot on the river where the bluffs swell like the crowns above an alligator's eyes. Just past the alligator's head, the shoreline loses its abruptness. On the north shore is the Landing, where the bare earth slopes gently to the river, and the earth beneath descends gradually. This is where our boats often make their entrances and exits. On the south shore is the Cotillion. Here the earth is hard as a dance floor; ancient cypresses, their full skirts sweeping across the shore, their arms raised, their lofty heads hopeful, wait for the embrace of lovers, wait patiently for the dance to begin.

River Caul

This is a stretch of river that some call the Straights of Behemoth. Others call the Tollbooth. The reason for the name stayed in the same spot for days, as though going for the world's water treading record. Its snout just above water, its rear legs hanging straight downward as though it were standing—one front leg was outstretched near the top of the water as though expecting a toll. No one claimed the floater. No one knew how it had died. No one could explain why it stayed in that spot so long, caught in what we thought must be a slow, eternal whirlpool, for whether you went upstream or down, the snout and the hollow eyes seemed fixed on you, as the outstretched leg waited for its toll. Seven feet below the river's surface, the serrated tail of the alligator disappeared into darkness. This the alligator that furnished the skull, which, now emblazoned with red and green eye socket transplants, glows at night in the Kicklighters' cabin.

Years after that suspended reptile finally decomposed enough to sink, we who know the river can still, if the sun is bright enough and correctly positioned, see the severed skeleton on the trunk of a fallen cypress near the river bottom.

The three men paddled to this spot. Diamond Jim, his head drooping, should have been able to see the skeleton. Should have, but he couldn't.

–Right there, his father said. If I jumped out of the boat I'd sink right on top of it. Can't you see? There?

We had always shrugged our shoulders at his inabilities. He would never know the river if he couldn't swim in it. It would forever withhold its treasures from him. For a moment those three men allowed themselves to feel sorry for the boy. His blonde hair stuck to the sweat on his forehead, though no one else was sweating; his eyes gazed down into the water and seemingly tried so hard to pick out the skeleton. They did feel sorry for him, a captive of his own fears, a captive of three men and of an entire community that would make of him something he was never intended to be, a community that would demand of his body and mind ransom he would never possess. Not only did his eyes look frightened and resigned, his flabby side, too, hung down. So for a moment they felt sorry for him even though in the same moment Raven read the shifts of the other two men and leaned his body with theirs, suspending themselves starboard. The hurried wide-eyed shift of the boy to port was not strong enough to counter. The boat, as planned, capsized. Among the last things they saw in that tumbling mix of sky, boat, faces, and water: the boy's pleading eyes.

We are always amazed when we read fictional accounts of people who fall unexpectedly into water. Paragraph after paragraph of slowly revolving prose, like the slowly revolving body struggling toward air. Five minutes of a body twirling through red-tinted water before gaining the surface and then swimming calmly to shore. Five minutes as though the lungs of the most able swimmer among us were so large and noble.

All three men spent their boyhoods in the river. There were days yet left in them when they could swim a half day back and forth, from shore to shore. Water was a home to them; they were confident in it. Even so, when the boat overturned, they reacted as though meeting water for the first time. They didn't tarry. They didn't spend minute after minute in underwater ballet, seeing in their revolutions the tops of shimmering trees. What they did was push the water with their hands, push down toward their feet as though the river were trousers to be shed quickly. They rushed to the surface and crossing that thin line their grateful mouths opened wide, their lungs feasted upon the sweet air.

The short while Raven was underwater, he didn't think of Diamond Jim, didn't wonder if the lesson had gone true to form and if alone and below the surface he had been able to find the swimming stroke that the best instructors had been trying to teach him, one that would work as well in water as on land. Raven didn't wonder if those wide, white tennis shoes, like weights, would sink Diamond Jim to the bottom or if he in panic would gulp water in the same way that Raven, upon surfacing, gulped air.

Raven swam away from the boat and retrieved his paddle. Only after he had the paddle in his hand, part of his transportation back to the cabin partially assured, did he wonder about Diamond Jim and his meeting with the river.

Three surfaced quickly. They pointed their paddles in triumph toward the sky.

–Wasn't so bad, Diamond Jim, was it? his father asked, swimming easily, then putting his arms on the keel of the boat, floating upside down twenty yards from the spot the toll keeper kept so long.

The time spent getting to the surface was a sudden moment, like the splash of rock in water. When the men got back to the boat and saw that Diamond Jim wasn't there, saw him nowhere in flow of river or on shore, that was an eternal moment, like a rock sinking slowly in a bottomless river.

It was his father who found him. The boy's white t-shirt and white tennis shoes looked much brighter than the bones of the alligator he lay beside. He was on his back, his side against the cypress log, a wedge that kept him from being dragged farther downstream. It took all three men to get him to the surface. His eyes, light blue like a hazy sky, were wide open, but what they had seen he never told.

Later, when the women arrived, the men didn't tell them that when they had arranged Diamond Jim on the sand so that his head was slightly downhill, better to drain the water from his lungs, Raven walked back into the river to retrieve the boat.

Generations

—Jesus, Raven, Doctor Kicklighter yelled, it doesn't matter. Let it go.

And so Raven came back and dropped to his knees in the sand beside Doctor Kicklighter, who was constantly checking Diamond Jim's pulse, and Diamond Jim's father, who pressed flat palms down hard on his son's back then rocked back and drew the boy's bent arms forward as though they were oars to row the river water from surfeited lungs.

Every movement on shore sounded of water. Their waterlogged clothes slogged. Water dropped from their bodies and splat into the sand and onto the soaked t-shirt, tight and transparent across the pale back of the boy. The odor of river seeped into their nostrils, and the fear of river, the fear they thought they had forgotten swept through their eyes.

—Fear or shame? Doctor Kicklighter would ask years later.

When the women arrived, they didn't ask anything. They went straight to the boy, still sprawled in the sand. Belly up, he waited, like a body on a gurney at Sim's Funeral Home.

Over Diamond Jim, the women huddled. This was how it must have been generations ago before we turned our dead over to morticians, before strangers prepared us for the grave. Then it was women—mothers, wives, sisters—who bathed the flesh. With their sensitive fingers feeling, with their hearts hoping for some stir of life. With grief and tenderness our limbs arranged as the women huddled over us.

Diamond Jim's mother brought his arms up over his belly. She rested her cheek against them while Betsy Kicklighter hurried with Raven's t-shirt to the river. When she returned, she wrung it out and handed it to the boy's mother. Her tender hands and wet cloth took the sand from his face. There was no threat, no condemnation in her eyes. He saw only love and concern. And so there in the sunlight with the women huddling over him, and the men backing away so their feet were in the river, a smile came back to his face.

When Diamond Jim graduated from high school, his parents bought him a new car. They parked it behind Dr. Kicklighter's office, so Diamond Jim wouldn't know about the surprise gift until after graduation. We might add that some of his classmates were given bass boats and ski boats by their parents.

Some of his peers, ones not graduating that night, some of the same ones who had laughed at him years before when he wouldn't splash with them in the wading pool, left the commencement ceremonies early and drove to Dr. Kicklighter's office.

When Diamond Jim saw his new Thunderbird, it had been customized. Streaks of soap had left the legend WATER BUG on the driver's door. A windshield-sized pair of goggles made out of black construction paper and a sheet of clear plastic glared out at the night. A large pair of flippers, made of cardboard, were attached to the car's rear bumper. When Diamond Jim saw the decorations he didn't laugh like the rest of us. Eighteen years old he was, and tears filled his eyes. His hands trembled as he ripped the accessories and threw them in disgust to the ground.

As far as any of us know that was the last indignity placed upon the boy. In fact, his fear of water had gone unstated by all of us from the red morning when he almost drowned until his graduation night.

The older we get, the more time we spend at the river. Now that Doctor Kicklighter is dead, and the cabin theirs alone, Raven and Betsy spend almost every weekend on the river. She says that there she can do her lesson plans in peace.

Raven finds at the river a suddenness that shakes him loose from boredom. The explosion might come from feathers as when

Generations

a flock of floating mallards is disturbed and so take themselves to air; the reverberations of the dark wings seem, for a moment, to empty his heart. But when their squadron is reformed and flies swiftly below the canopy of trees, his heart is filled with richer, cleaner blood.

Sometimes the suddenness is from memory, like the afternoon on the deck jutting out over the river when Betsy asked: Raven, do you feel responsible for what happened?

—Godamighty, Betsy. He was sprawled out one night right where your feet are now, kicking his by-God feet in the air like he was going to be able to swim the next by-God day when his father and my father and me turned the by-God boat over and dumped him...

—Raven, there's no need to *by God*.

—Well then, I feel no more responsible than anyone else, mortal or divine.

Don't think what happened to Diamond Jim was sudden like the fright that ignites the mallards and sends them blasting from the water. Reaction makes them take to wing. What finally made Diamond Jim take to the water on his own was learning, not reaction.

When Betsy spreads out her lessons plans: objective, materials, procedure, we are amazed. How ridiculous, really, we think, to believe that she can plan a strategy that will teach anything in one day. Do we learn that quickly?

We thought all our efforts had been lost. We didn't know that all those years, all those times we told Diamond Jim that if he would be of us, he must be water, for water is us, Diamond Jim was taking those lessons to heart. When he left in WATER BUG for a landlocked college, we didn't know he would stop on the highway, get out of the car and talk aloud to himself. Diamond Jim could have continued the way he was going, away from river, but instead he got back in the car and drove to the Landing, to the north shore where the land slopes slowly beneath the river, and where on the opposite shore, the Cotillion, the full-skirted cypresses wait for the music to begin.

There were a few of us around, but no one stayed on the river long that day. The wind was out of the north and the water too unsettled for fishing. Whitecaps, rare for our river, rose above the normally smooth surface. Upstream and down, as far as eye could see, white turmoil warned us: stay away. So all we ever got is bits and pieces of what must have happened.

Raven, seeing him emptying his pockets near the top of the ramp, pulled up and talked to him awhile. Said Diamond Jim looked the best he had ever seen him, seemed calm and rational.

—I just stopped by for a look before I make the long drive, he told Raven.

—Maybe you better look from your car.

That was the last Raven ever saw of Diamond Jim. Though few of us saw him that day, we have that memory of him, for at some point in his life we all saw him like that: water before him, his feet planted firmly on land.

Days, sometimes even years go by, and all is calm as though the river had had enough of rising and falling and had found contentment. Then there are other times so noticeably different that we wouldn't be surprised if the river left its banks and crawled up the cypresses and swarmed over every limb and leaf, while from the crowns, great rushes of water shot upwards like fountains. It's those days that, as Raven Kicklighter says: You, by God, watch the river and listen to its every shout and murmur.

Something happened that day. A suddenness came to all the years of lessons. One of us saw Diamond Jim take off his shoes, roll up his pants and walk down the concrete ramp. Another said Diamond Jim waved as he stood knee-deep in the river. Whitecaps brushed against his thighs; the wind blew so strong it looked like it had him by his blonde hair and was leading him

Generations

deeper into the water. We, of course, don't know precisely how it went, but as much as we know of water we bet we're not far off.

He went in the river because how could he start a new life if he had never lived the old one? How could he ever expect to be a part of a new community like a college, if he had never grabbed hold of the river and its community? He waded in, not to drown himself, but to know himself. He wanted a moment of suspension in water, of being in control of himself in water. We hoped that, at least for a moment, he found that valid swimming stroke that had eluded him for so long, that at least for a moment he moved about joyfully in the windswept current. That's what we still hope. But what we know is: he looked landward; water and fright swept across his face. Though he flailed the water with his large, powerful arms, he never broke the caul of river.

Mrs. Dickens Goes to the Drugstore

They're almost gone now, like grocery stores with screen doors, like hardware stores with warped, deep-scratched wooden floors, gone...like men who tipped their hats to ladies; gone, too, the ladies who appreciated and acknowledged such antiquated gestures; gone, women who allowed themselves to be called ladies, women who used Mrs. before their names; gone, too, the kids who called them Misries, after the fashion of the day. Extinct. The classic kind. Social drugstores. The ones with "Doc" in the back translating medical hieroglyphics into bottles of cures; drugstores, where behind marble fountains, "jerks" added flavors of vanilla and cherry to Cokes, which were served in thin glasses shaped like upside down Bartlett pears, jerks pulling handles at the fountain, shaking by hand the milk, ice cream, and malt, listening and watching as in the booths, at the tables, and on the worn leather stools around the fountain the town's most important business was transacted: marriages, births, sicknesses, and deaths announced; shops bought and sold before the mugs of cooling coffee; gossip scooped up like ice cream and spooned into hungry mouths; stories, like sterling silver, polished and laid out for special occasions.

But one of the ladies remembers, remembers when the indented circles on the floor were more secure than impressions, remembers when bolts held the bases of the stools secure, when

Generations

the twisted wooden dowels that decorate the empty mirror were polished once a week, when the cantilevered glass case that juts from the mirror was filled with cakes and pies and sweets rolls and how the sugary smell of a bakery filled her nostrils each time the creaky glass door opened, remembers, too, when the message on the chalkboard in her own dining room was freshened every Monday. When that board called her out of the darkness of solitude and into friendship's rich light.

It's two o'clock in the afternoon. Mrs. Octavia Reeves and dust rag move quietly and familiarly among the relics of her kitchen. Mrs. Reeves is dusting time away. She is careful that she doesn't disturb the chalkboard, on which she has printed: 3PM. MEET MRS. MCKINNON AND MRS. DICKENS AT THE DRUGSTORE. TREAT THEM WITH KINDNESS. The message, anointed with fresh chalk once a week, has been there for years.

—Mrs. McKinnon, she says to the chalkboard, I don't know why you and Mrs. Dickens are insisting that I bring my glasses today. You know I don't like to wear those ugly things in public. Oh, I do hate to wear the things. Why are you so insistent?

Mrs. Reeves used to think of many things in the hour before three, but now, it seems, she thinks only of the drugstore and her friends, of light and laughter and hope, of that glittering mirror behind the marble fountain that draws her each day out of a lonely house that seems to her much too much like a grave.

Blue tint highlighting their white hair, they sit on stools at the end of the counter. Rouge is heavy on their cheeks, and around them hovers an air of perfume, as though bath powder were still settling. Their dresses are neatly ironed; their hose clean and

Mrs. Dickens Goes to the Drugstore

without runs. They hold their pocketbooks in their laps and prop braceleted arms on the marble counter.

—Oh, thank you, Mrs. Reeves says as a cup is placed before her. You haven't worked here long, but you're learning our habits. She pauses, then asks in a quieter voice: Now what does Mrs. Dickens want today? Mrs. Reeves laughs.

—The usual, right? Mrs. McKinnon answers for her.

—She never eats anything. Before long she'll be no bigger than a minute, Mrs. Reeves sighs jokingly.

The soda fountain girl wipes a wet strand of hair behind her ear with one hand as she pours coffee with the other. She knows to keep these thoughts unspoken: *Learning your habits? The whole town has known your habits for years. I think you're crazy.*

Mrs. Reeves glances at the girl. Constantly on the lookout for changes, she checks the top of the mirror to see if the crack has lengthened. Relieved that it hasn't, she motions the fountain girl over.

—Doesn't Mrs. McKinnon have pretty eyes? You can really see them when she takes her glasses off. I hate glasses. Make you look bad. Can't wear a hat. Make you look like the dickens. Oh excuse me, Mrs. Dickens.

—Would you please be careful when you pour us more coffee? We don't want to mess up the picture.

Mrs. McKinnon centers the picture on the counter and tries to get Mrs. Reeves to notice.

—You haven't seen it since I had it touched up. Look at it with your glasses on. Have you seen it with your glasses on?

—Oh, I hate to wear the things, Mrs. Reeves says. They rub blisters behind your ears, gouge out the bridge of your nose. Jim's nose got so bad before he died. I filled those two spots with natural color wood putty one afternoon while he slept. Scared Jim silly when he sat up. Thought his eyes had fallen out. I just hate glasses.

Generations

    –Don't sit there dangling your glasses. Put them on. I want you to see how pretty she looks.
    –Yes, yes, she says, holding her glasses with one hand and the picture with the other, it's good to see the color in her cheeks again. Mrs. Reeves puts her glasses down. Tell me what you been doing today. You listening, Mrs. Dickens?
    –Ironing curtains, Mrs. McKinnon says. I been ironing curtains all day. They're like husbands. You think you got one pressed down and figured out and then an unexpected ruffle flops out at you.
    –Oh, Mrs. Dickens, I remember how you used to look in ruffles. You weren't *one* of the pretty girls, Mrs. Reeves says, pressing the hand of the soda fountain girl to detain her, you were *the* pretty girl. Pretty as this one here.
    –That's the truth, Mrs. Dickens. And such a figure. Eat anything and never get fat. Have two milkshakes while Mrs. Reeves and I would split ours.
    They can tell the girl has taken about all of their talk she can, so Mrs. Reeves releases the girl's hand.
    –We've got to work on that little hussy. She treats us like we're nothing. And Mrs. McKinnon, I want to compliment you on the way you let Mrs. Dickens and me in on the conversation yesterday. It wasn't so one-sided, and I want you to know that Mrs. Dickens and I were proud of you. I appreciated the way you let Mrs. Dickens have her story. You know she'll go the longest time in silence, like a leaf pressed away in a book.
    –Hold your ears. I'm about to awaken this little thing from the dead.
    Mrs. McKinnon captures the girl's attention and begins quietly: Peterson Avenue wasn't like it is now with all those cars and trucks whizzing by. The street wasn't even paved, and there was a statue right in the middle.

Mrs. Dickens Goes to the Drugstore

—The courthouse across the street wasn't so square and ugly. The one we knew as girls had spires and turrets. It looked like a fancy birthday cake sitting under the sun, Mrs. Reeves adds.

Mrs. McKinnon waits till the girl has turned away from them, then shouts, *It burned down!*

A glass falls from the hand of the startled girl and shatters on the floor.

—Don't you worry about that, Mrs. McKinnon says. There was a day when the three of us gave away cases of old Mr. Thompson's glassware.

Leaning toward Mrs. McKinnon, Mrs. Reeves muffles her voice to a whisper: She needs to know all this.

—We watched the fire from the porch, Mrs. Reeves says quietly to the girl.

—Yes, Mrs. McKinnon continues, the drugstore still had a porch then. A porch lined with rocking chairs.

—You might not believe it, Mrs. Reeves says, but we were schoolgirls once. We'd walk here every afternoon after school.

—The boys leaned forward in those chairs trying to get a better look at us. I don't mean polite leaned, Mrs. McKinnon says emphatically to the girl, I mean bowing 'bout to their knees and grinning.

—I'm glad I don't fall in love as easy as I did then, Mrs. Reeves says, leaving the sugar out of her second cup of coffee.

—We'd walk across the drugstore porch extra slow. Let them wonder if we were going in or were we going to sit in the rocking chairs.

—Davis Drugstore was across the street.

—This town was connected by drugstores then.

—A block from here, we'd walk pass McRae's Drugstore.

—And we'd always look up at those gargoyles on the bank.

—When you're young....

Generations

–You look up at those opened mouths and imagine there are monsters in the world.
–And when you get older, Mrs. Reeves says, you know there are.
–Mrs. Dickens's oldest son hugged and kissed Mr. and Mrs. Dickens right here in the drugstore.
–The last place they saw him before he went back.
–And nine months later he was dead on Omaha Beach.
–Couldn't bring his body back. Buried him right in the crater left by the shell.
–But Mrs. Dickens didn't miss a day at the drugstore.
–You see she had to be strong for us. We had sons over there, too.
–Oh, Mrs. McKinnon says, it's taking us too long to get around the block. Let's hurry back to our drugstore.

The ladies turn and grin at each other. They press their arms down on the marble counter. Lock their eyes on the fountain girl's and pump their arms like sprinters. The girl hears the clang of their bracelets, hears their feet tapping out rapid strides on the marble curb. Watches them giggle as their faces turn red with the continuation of their pretend run. The girl closes her eyes.

–After school the porch would be full of handsome boys and young men waiting to see who'd be the first one to buy a shake for Mrs. Dickens that day.
–Now you know that's the truth, Mrs. Dickens, they both say.

The girl turns away.

It's not the same without an audience. They grow silent, slowly sipping the last of their coffees, reluctant to reach the bottom. The crowd has really slimmed down. Their crowd. Yet memories hold them, frozen, immobile like the marble countertop.

Mrs. Dickens Goes to the Drugstore

Looking at their reflections in the mirror, timing the moment the girl will turn back toward them, Mrs. Reeves says: I remember when her daughter died. She points to Mrs. Dickens so the girl will know.

The ladies pause; they watch the fountain girl to see if she will move toward them or lean back.

–There's lots about this town we know, about life, too.

–We got it all in our heads.

The fountain girl looks incredulous, then blinks until disbelief yields to the familiar comfort of boredom.

–Yes, your daughter's death was a rough time for you, wasn't it Mrs. Dickens?

–When your children go to war, you know they're wearing danger day and night.

–But when your eight-year-old daughter is swinging in her own backyard, leaning back with her long hair sweeping down toward the ground...

–Her belly quivering with laughter...

–And she stretches out a bare foot to touch a pear blossom...

–You don't expect the rope to break.

–Back then, Gaskin Avenue wasn't paved. Palm trees lined both sides of the street from Walker Street to the cemetery.

–Made the day seem especially stately and sad. The way the palm trees...

–Dipped and swayed in the wind....

–As though the funeral procession moved along an avenue of long-haired daughters swinging.

–After that, Mrs. Dickens sat alone in her bedroom, shades drawn, curtains pinned together. Wouldn't come out for weeks after her daughter's death.

–You can't take a friend's hurt away.

–You can't live the pain for her either.

–But you can be there when grief starts to give way.

Generations

   –That was me and Mrs. Reeves. Standing on the street corner outside Mrs. Dickens's house. Every day regular as Mister Mingledoff delivering the mail.
   –The wait wasn't done in a week.
   –Wasn't done in a month.
   –A season passed is what it was.
   –Till there came a summer day we stood fanning ourselves on the corner. At 2:45 like always.
   –And the curtain in Mrs. Dickens's room pulled back, just a tad.
   –Wasn't no more than taking a strand of your hair and parking it behind your ear.
   –Just a hair that curtain moved.
   –And oh didn't we move. Me and Mrs. Reeves boogied up to the doorbell. Didn't you know, I told Mrs. Dickens so soft, that when you pulled back that curtain you'd see us? Don't you know, we're not the only thing been missing you?
   –Every afternoon we went by. Told her how much we loved her. Told her we were going to the drugstore and if she wanted to come along she was welcome.
   –More than welcome.
   –And finally one day she said, 'It might do me some good, but...'
   –We didn't give her time to finish *butting* 'cause we grabbed her by the arms.
   –One of us on each side...
   –And brought her here.
   –She took the tiniest steps until she was under the gargoyles.
   –Then her stride picked up.
   –Oh, that lady had the sweetest little run then.
   –Went so fast she was sitting at the counter while Mrs. Reeves and I were getting to the rocking chairs.

Mrs. Dickens Goes to the Drugstore

—She finished two shakes, just like that, and we were afraid she'd want to go on back home.

—So we ordered another shake apiece, to delay, you see.

—I started getting fat that day, Mrs. Reeves sighs. I told Jim before he died that if Mrs. Dickens's daughter could of stayed alive I never would of been a fat woman.

—But it did help Mrs. Dickens to come back to the drugstore.

—Cured her, sure as we're sitting here. She went home that afternoon—didn't you Mrs. Dickens?—undid those curtains, let those shades up a little. Never did draw her room in that much darkness again.

For a moment, the girl stares at them; they smile back, grateful for the recognition. The girl once more sweeps a strand of hair behind her head. She is wondering when she'll hear from one of the fast-food restaurants. She longs to work at a place where people sit away from the counter, where she won't have to listen to breathy old stories.

—Do you know, Mrs. Reeves asks the girl, that the three of us: that's me, she points to herself and then to the lady next to her, Mrs. McKinnon...

—Hello, Mrs. McKinnon says, laughing.

—And Mrs. Dickens have been coming here for seventy-five years?

—The drugstore opened on Mrs. Dickens's sixth birthday.

—Her mother brought us here for the party.

—We were ornery. None of us wanted to wear dresses.

—And Mrs. Dickens was downright mean, weren't you, honey?

—Her little brother was about three months old, and she was still so jealous of him.

—I noticed the little baby draw down on his nose when he was breathing. He was struggling and trying to widen his nostrils.

Generations

–When Mrs. Dickens' mother turned him toward sunlight, you would have swore roots were growing out his nose.

–Mrs. Dickens' mother left us under the watchful eyes of Mr. Thompson and rushed that baby down to Doctor Kicklighter's office.

–Oh, she was mad when she came back.

–See, about a week before, Mrs. Dickens had stuffed a black-eyed pea up each nostril.

–She didn't tell anybody about it.

–But seeds will tell. Those seeds germinated.

–Doctor Kicklighter laughed all over town a week over that one.

–Said if he knew the Dickens were that short of growing space, he'd of shared his garden.

–That was three-quarters of a century ago; we haven't missed a day in the last fifty years. Me and Mrs. Reeves haven't. Not even the days of our husbands' funerals.

–They wanted us to come here afterwards.

–Knew about our attendance...

–Streak. Better go, Jim said.

–Their deaths weren't unexpected, but Mrs. Dickens's daughter was so young, wasn't she, honey?

–The death of her daughter put a gap in Mrs. Dickens's streak.

–Never knew we'd keep at it so long, says Mrs. McKinnon, because it didn't seem that important to us when the streak began.

–I agree, says Mrs. Reeves, and Mrs. Dickens does, too. It didn't seem no more to us than putting a penny in those old weight and fortune scales that used to stand right outside the door.

The fountain girl sighs and shifts from foot to foot.

Mrs. Dickens Goes to the Drugstore

–I don't remember when we changed our way of thinking about the drugstore. It might have been the first year or might have been the tenth.

–I sure remember, Mrs. Reeves says quickly. For me it was when I realized my life was like a Coke being pulled from the fountain. I knew I wasn't going to fizz forever.

–Lord, God. When you stop fizzing, they might as well throw me away, too.

The ladies lock arms and stare past the girl at their pale reflections in the mirror.

–Do you remember how pretty we were? Mrs. McKinnon asks. How we could make that mirror smile?

–I remember that a little bit, Mrs. Reeves says. But look at us now. We look like things too old to keep, but too ugly to put in a museum. Except for you, of course, Mrs. Dickens. Mrs. Reeves pats the photo apologetically. Oh, Mrs. Dickens, do you remember the day the War ended?

–The *Big One*, Mrs. McKinnon yells at the fountain girl. World War II.

–The horns blasting in the street.

–I can still hear them. The three of us jumped from our stools…

–And went to dancing on the counter.

–More like a promenade.

–It was a strut. That's what it was. With Mrs. Dickens leading us. She'd go down to the end of the counter there, throw her arms up, and shake her fanny. Then strut back down this way weaving between us.

–Then right down there she'd be shaking her fanny again.

–If our husbands could of seen us that day they would of traded us in on government bonds.

–We were all laughing. Mrs. Dickens, too. But there was hurt in her laugh.

Generations

—You didn't hear it, but you knew it had to be there. The war was over for us. For Mrs. Dickens and her son, it never ended.

—I don't even remember going home that day. All I remember is being here at the drugstore with my dear, dear friends. I can still see Mrs. Dickens jump down from the counter and start slinging bowl after bowl of vanilla ice cream.

—And handing them to me, says Mrs. Reeves, so I could glob some chocolate sauce on top.

—And me running to the door giving bowls to people passing on the street. And Mr. Thompson running after me, yelling: It's all right you give away my ice cream, but don't give away my store, too.

—He was laughing.

—Oh, we've been so happy here in this drugstore, and sometimes for no other reason than being together.

—We'll keep coming even when we're down to one.

Mrs. McKinnon reaches into her pocketbook. You haven't seen this, she says to the girl. Here's the picture of Mrs. Dickens's grave.

Sick, Sick, Sick, Sick, the girl thinks. How long's she been dead? the girl asks. Earl Lee Thompson, Jr. had told her to act interested in them. Humor them, he had said, it's part of your job.

—Dead. How long? the girl prompts wearily.

—Her youngest son called and told us they were having the funeral at three o'clock.

—Didn't tell us, says Mrs. McKinnon, asked us if three would be okay.

—He said I know you and my mother have been meeting at the drugstore at three o'clock for years, but with relatives from out of town and all, it seems like afternoon…

Mrs. Dickens Goes to the Drugstore

—We didn't let him finish. Told him that for decades everything important in her life had started at three.

—We came here right after the funeral.

—Brought a picture of her.

—And were still here crying when old Mr. Thompson told us he was sorry, but he did have to close the store.

—Told us he'd lock us in, and we could stay overnight if we wanted.

—We'll keep coming to this drugstore. We've agreed the last one will bring pictures of the others, sit here and sip for old times' sake.

—And try to smile like we've always smiled in here. But it will be so hard, Mrs. McKinnon says, reaching for Mrs. Reeves's hand. It will be so empty.

—I told Jim before he died that if I'm the last one left then whoever's working the fountain can pour my milkshake into a thimble because that's about all I'd have the stomach for. Mrs. Reeves sighs and shakes her head. It'll be five years next week, but Mrs. Dickens can keep coming to the drugstore with us if she wants to. She's such a sweet lady.

—Yes, says Mrs. McKinnon, putting Mrs. Dickens back into her pocketbook, it does her so much good to come here with us. She does so love to go to the drugstore.

—She loves to because tomorrow will be so different. That's what makes the drugstore so exciting for the three of us.

—Before you go, Mrs. McKinnon reminds, spin around three times and say you love me and Mrs. Dickens.

—I love you both, Mrs. Reeves says quietly.

—I love you both, too, Mrs. McKinnon says, finishing her last revolution. If my blood pressure don't go down, we'll have to think of some other way.

Generations

—It's been good chatting with you, Mrs. Reeves says, patting the hand of the fountain girl. And Mrs. McKinnon and Mrs. Dickens, I look forward to seeing you again tomorrow.

At the door, Mrs. Dickens, secure in Mrs. McKinnon's pocketbook, pauses with her friends as they look back at the fountain. The ladies smile; Mrs. Reeves waves to the girl at the fountain, but the girl doesn't see her. The errant strand of hair flops across the girl's eyes as she scrubs the black marble, polishing away their prints.

A Promise for George Washington Gonzales

—What's wrong with everybody? Juan Gonzales asked, slamming his fist down. With grumpy Flora, with the boy.

—He knows, Flora replied deliberately, that other families get what they promise themselves. Then he sees us. He has too long heard me talk about my little house, my flowers. But we stay in this apartment. Years are much longer to him than to us, and he thinks never will we have those things, never will we have anything but talk. Now that you've taken the money out of the bank, she said, turning away, who knows what might happen.

Juan looked out the window at the used car lot and service station where he worked. On the other side of their apartment was the jail. A busy street. Not a good place to raise a family. Not a good place to live long, yet they had lived there eight years, saving a little money month by month, year by year.

—He would like the Cadillac, eh? A new car for our boy.

—No. I've talked to him. He thinks it's foolish to spend all that money on just a car. After all these years, we can finally touch a dream. A dream, Juan. Not two.

—You think a car is foolish, and you make him think it.

—You are good with cars; you can keep the one we have now running and running. He likes your car; he doesn't mind that it is old.

Generations

 —Eh, he's a good boy, a smart boy.
 —Very intelligent and well liked. We are lucky.
 —But he will not get much without determination.
 —He has that. He is fierce like you.
 —No, he's sad, Flora. He thinks his old man cannot do what he promised he would do. Let's get the fine, big car now.
 —You promised him? Flora asked.
 —Yes, Juan said and once more looked down at the street. In spite of Flora's confidence in him, he couldn't keep a car running forever. He hadn't that night eight years before.
 —Remember how people laughed when I pushed our car into the station while you big-bellied pregnant walked alongside. I promised our son that night, a month before he was born, that one day we would have a new car, bright as a sunrise, and people would not laugh at us. I've told him of that promise. I told him again today.
 —And I promised him a house. We will have a better, quieter place to live, a place where we can grow our own vegetables and plant our own trees. We can start that tomorrow, Juan, so that one day we will have peppers we pick from our own garden, peaches we pick from our own trees. Our place: George's, Juan's, Flora's. Ours. In the United States. The new car can wait. Maybe when you own the station. You are no longer the poor migrant who must dream of flashy cars.
 —But our son must dream.
 —He does. He thinks he will be a scientist or a writer or painter, he says *painter*. He says *pintar*. He knows two languages; he wants to learn more. He knows hope, and he knows to dream. Already he is reaching.
 —That's why we must have the car for our son. I can feel his spirit riding my shoulders like a bird rides the wind. If I soar, he will soar. If he doesn't see me riding high, he will never fly.

A Promise for George Washington Gonzalez

—That's foolish, Flora said and turned toward a sound. George Washington Gonzales was sitting on the floor, his back resting against the doorjamb. A pencil had fallen from his hand.
—When did you come in? Flora asked.
—I never went out.
—We'll go now, Juan said. I must have a talk with my son.

They sat on wood crates under a streetlight. In their apartment window a small pine tree silvered with tinsel supported strings of blinking lights. Next year, Flora had said as they decorated the tree, we'll have a bigger one, in our own house, by our own window.

Juan closed his eyes and imagined Flora smiling beside the tree in the house she wanted; then he opened them and imagined a big, new car sitting in the parking space beneath their apartment's Christmas tree. The boy stared at the tree. Cars rushed past; a traffic light switched back and forth.

—This year has been good for us, Juan began. We can finally have that big Christmas we have long talked of. We can buy a small house, or we can buy a big fine car. He leaned forward. Which do you want?

The boy looked down.
—Which? Juan repeated.
The boy sighed. The house, I think.
—Why?
—Mama thinks it will be better for us in our own house.
—And you would like that?
—Yes.
—And you don't want the car?
—I would like us to have both.
—But you think the car can wait?
—Mama says...

Generations

–George Washington Gonzales, what do you think?

–I think the car would be very nice, he giggled.

–Very nice is right, Juan said. Unless the wind blows very hard a house cannot move; it isn't a traveler or a teacher. It isn't temperamental like a car. It isn't spirited. Besides, he grinned and leaned closer to his son, if you grease a house, you get fussed at. Come, Juan said. I have the money with me.

He led the boy down the street to Fender's Cadillac. In the showroom three new Cadillacs gleamed. The one that captured their attention most had a black top and a metallic gold body.

–Oh we would look rich in that, Juan said. Black to match our hair.

–And the gold will look like we're wearing gold pants, the boy said.

–It's a beauty, no? We would be very important in that car.

–It's beautiful, he agreed and saw in his father's eyes the same look the house evoked in his mother's.

–I can get the car now, but there will be no money left for a house. He placed his hand on his son's thick hair.

–Your momma is right. Her choice is logical and wise. Mine is foolish. She will be angry with me if I do what I want to do. She will hate me for awhile. And I'll be angrier with myself if I don't. A man must do something big for himself or he has no respect. A woman must have some wish come true or else life is empty. What's a man to do?

–Maybe a man has to decide which is better, the boy said.

–Hey, Juan said. I'm not trying to make your momma unhappy. If I could reach the heavens I'd pluck her a star.

–She'd rather have a house, the boy said.

–Did you get it? Flora asked as they walked in the door.

–What? Juan asked.

–The car. It was the car you left for. Did you buy it?

A Promise for George Washington Gonzalez

Looking at his fingers, scarred from years of salvaging old engines, Flora knew how much he deserved a new car, but she couldn't bear to hear the *yes*.

—Eh, Juan said. That is a big problem. You promised him the house because you think that best; I promise the car for the same reason. For love, we promise two different things.

—Because you two can't agree, the boy said, let me choose which promise we will have.

—How would you do that? Flora asked.

—Would you pick what your mama wants? Juan asked, gently turning the boy's head toward Flora. Or what your father wants?

—I would choose for George Washington Gonzales and his family.

Because Flora didn't think it fair that their son be burdened with the entire decision, they each went into separate rooms to write their choices. Flora and Juan finished quickly and put their folded papers on the living room floor and then watched their son as he stared out the window by the Christmas tree. Looking at him sitting thoughtfully in the large chair, Flora said: He is so little to make such a big decision.

Impatient after five minutes, she called out to him.

—It will take me awhile to decide what is best, he said. Will you give me that time?

—Eh, the little kid is smart, Juan said. We were migrants too long, Flora. We picked tomatoes, peaches, oranges, beans. As children we were groundhogs, walking on our hands and knees, gathering the fallen fruit from the earth. We picked with our fingers. Grabbed fast. Walk about on your knees sometimes, being a groundhog, picking the fallen fruit. With your fingers you pick a house. With my fingers I pick. Our son picks with his brain. Smarter, but takes longer. Give the boy time.

After an hour, Juan called out: Hey, boy. Your brain go to sleep?

Generations

–I'm closer, the boy said.

Flora shook the papers in the palm of her hand, then let three pieces fall to the table. She opened hers first and showed "HOUSE" to her family. The paper to her right with the big loose fold was Juan's. She picked the tightly, neatly folded one instead. "House," it said. The boy smiled weakly at his father.

–There are already two for the house, Flora said. There was no gloating in her voice. It was soft, subdued, sad. Your choice will have to wait.

–It isn't fair not to count it.

Flora nodded. You deserve your choice, too, Juan, Flora said as she held the paper. Maybe in a few more years.

–Eh, maybe my choice is to show I have a brain, too. That I can pick with my head and with my heart. I learn that from my son, no. Learn to be smart.

Juan and the boy leaned toward Flora's hands as she unwrapped the paper on which Juan had written: HOUSE OF THE GONZALES.

The boy smiled up at his father.

Dust

The family always sat in front. Jacob, a nickname given because of a childhood habit of climbing pews, sat in the second pew. His cousin and his cousin's wife sat in front of him. In the sunlight filtering in through the stained glass, the dust motes hung suspended.

At his cousin's wedding, Jacob had been the ring bearer, with long white coattails dragging across the carpet, while in his hands he held an ornate cushion of red felt with golden spines. "What God has joined together…," the minister had said after the rings were lifted.

When he became a teenager, acutely aware of the flesh, Jacob developed an admiration for the couple. Partly because they were both handsome, but mainly because they were in love. Even with all its contradictions, love fascinated him. It was fragile, yet strong; within grasp, but elusive; common yet so rare.

He watched a succession of ministers preach of love: God's love for humankind, a mother's love for her child, a husband's for his wife. While ministers changed, the couple sat steadily on the front row through the years of Sundays. Sometimes they giggled; sometimes joined hands, even sprouted gray hair together, but always they sat shoulder to shoulder.

But not this Sunday. Jacob saw their shoulders were slightly apart; a shiver ran through his body as though something deep inside him, some instinct, some belief, some certainty had been severed. He looked around to see if anyone else had noticed. His father sat, as usual, with head inclined, his mother with forefinger pressed into cheek. Between Jacob and the stained-glass window, the dust motes swirled.

Each week after that, the distance between shoulders increased until one Sunday Jacob's cousin sat in church alone, listing slightly to the right as though to press the phantom shoulder. Jacob felt the hurt.

—God knows your pain and sorrow, the minister was saying, and how like death separation is. But he gave you tear ducts so you could cry. He gave you eyes and a brain that you might see and learn. Feet and courage that you might walk beyond despair. God joins, but staying together is our choice.

In the sunlight the dust motes rose and lowered softly. Jacob watched as two came from a distance, danced around the others, touched, then parted.

Mockingbird

Robert Vickers was the fourth generation of his family to conjure crops from the Georgia sand. At seventy-nine, large and red-faced with thin lips, gaps in uneven rows of yellowed teeth, and age lines that ran like streams down his face, he'd reached the age where man uses the ancient pump of his heart for shallow schemes. He had once hoped to buy surrounding farms and improve them with the labor of sons and grandsons. Yet he had never married and had barely managed keeping his inherited farm. Where he had once hoped to see the entire farm fenced, he had settled on doing the three large fields. He was on the last one now, the largest one, but had strayed far from his work. His tractor, with auger raised, was parked in the pines at the edge of the field. Rolls of barbed wire, marking the corners, heated in the sunlight, and creosoted posts lay in the field.

    Robert leaned his sweaty back against the trunk of the white oak tree in the middle of the field and measured his progress along the perimeter. Posts were upright and tamped on three sides and the fourth was half done. The old man relaxed, listening to the staccato song of a mockingbird perched high in the tree and watching the haze and ripple of heat waves borne skyward.

    He had spent many noons under the shade with his father while their horses cropped grass with a pleasant, rhythmic

Generations

clamping of grinders and an occasional stomp of rear hoofs to dislodge pesky flies. Alwin Vickers had been a large man, too, with a reputation for being hard and vain. The old woman in the cabin by the field knew it, her son knew it. Robert agreed with the assessment. He'd seen his father shoot a mule for balking, and many times under the tree, he'd seen the vanity, watched him take a rag, wipe the sand from his boots, then grease them with tallow from the small can he kept in his pocket, prop them on the log positioned slightly beyond the overhang of the oak so he could lie in the shadow of noon and keep an eye on his tenant farmers while his boots glistened in the sun. Those boots had a sun-blessed sheen the day Robert, aged fourteen, carried the left leg home, ran past the white oak with the surprisingly heavy leg of his father balanced across his shoulder; he held it by the shin, the tallow rank at close quarters and the leather thongs double-knotted with a neat bow, which flapped like twin nooses.

In a corner of the field, then as now, stood a house. Age had diminished the frame structure. A porch and bedroom in disrepair had been dismantled, leaving a kitchen and bedroom. The two people who lived there were guaranteed a free house as long as Robert Vickers lived.

Inside, Bird Williams tended the small fire on the sunken floor of the fireplace, which had been forged by years of its own heat into a vast, black bowl, blacker even than his own skin. The thin white curtains in the room were dingy. On the walls were faded photographs pasted into shoe box tops, which hung like framed paintings. One bed was in the corner of the room, and the other, in which his mother stayed, was near the fireplace. She was ninety-two, blind, and always cold. Shaded by the chinaberry tree, a used bedpan waited on the windowsill.

–What's Robert doing now? she asked.

–Last I saw, he was leaning 'gainst the white oak.

–How far's he come?

Mockingbird

–'Bout half-way to us.

–I don't like it a tall. He's got no right.

–It's his field, Momma. White folks' land. Ain't a black owns farmland in this whole county.

–Lord, boy, I don't want nothing fencing me in. I ain't running nowhere. That old tree ain't running nowhere.

–I hear you, Momma.

–Don't need no barbed wire. They's enough already to stick you in this country. Her thin body shook with a long, guttural laugh. If you can get past the stinging nettle, the blackberry gonna get you, or the pine needles or wasps, mosquitoes or ticks, chiggers, one of them rattlesnakes what's in ever palmetto fan, and, Lord, if you get past all that and you're young enough, the prickly heat will jump outta the bushes and gnaw on you.

–You hush up talking. Gonna get too excited if you go on like that. Way I remember it, you was always one who liked being out with the blackberries and chiggers.

–Never liked no rattlesnake, or white snake neither. I'm telling you the truth, child. Telling you the truth.

–Sweet Jesus, you are.

–Now, she said, rubbing her dry, loose lips, I hear a mockingbird in that oak.

–Don't go hearing no mockingbird on me, Momma.

–Can't help it, child. I hear it singing low, singing sweet, I hear it. Heard it last night, too. Mockingbird knows something.

–I been hearing you talk about 'em for sixty-five years, he said as he moved to her side. Ain't no mockingbird out there today. Ain't none a tall. Don't tell me 'bout no mockingbird.

In 1915 when she first told him about the mockingbird, she seemed so tall to him, and fleshy, though not fat. Stately in her prime. Working as he did, hoeing cotton and corn, Bird was aware of the health of things. It was something he saw in the

Generations

fields after a rain, the way the crops pushed harder toward maturity. It was in the lungs of Bird and his friends racing through a newly-turned field before the seeds were dropped. Reverberating in a man's shout, a woman's singing, health was not timid. Whether it swaggered like the boy who won the race, or leaned gently like a plant toward sunlight, health kept a visible countenance. It was in the green of the fields and the brown of his mother as she sat on the porch, her skirt pulled up to her thighs, and her trim legs warming in the afternoon light. Ain't no man can warm me like that Mr. Sun, she'd say with a grin. Her pronouncement didn't keep men from trying.

Some nights, Bird lay awake and listened to the voice of a man in his mother's room. There was a pattern. The man would come in laughing and talking loud, shaking the cabin like a storm; then things would quieten and get peaceful like a gentle rain on the tin roof, and Bird would almost go to sleep. But the calm was only the eye of the storm. Moans would swell up out of the room, and the bed would crash against the wall as though someone was slamming it from one side of the room to the other. Bird would sit up on his pallet, his heart beating wildly.

Once, while his brother and sister slept on the floor of the unheated room, Bird crawled to the door and tugged at the bottom until he stretched the door far enough from the twine latch to get a partial view of his mother's room. On the floor beside her bed, a man's pants had crumpled into a heap. A gold chain dangled from the watch fob and glittered in the firelight; the ticking of the watch was audible. Next to the pants stood a pair of sturdy boots smeared with tallow.

Bird was fascinated by the bare legs, which he could see from the calves down. They were large legs, matted with thick black hair, yet they seemed so pale, so white. The hair came down to a black dagger point stopping almost even with the ankles. Then, at once, the feet were no longer there, vanished from Bird's sight

Mockingbird

as though sprung to heaven accompanied by a penetrating thud and the loud slamming of the bed. The edges of the quilt jerked up and down like cloth puppets.

–No, not tonight, no. Unh unh.

–Leave her alone, Bird shouted.

–You hush up, Bird, his mother said. I's alright.

Bird clawed at the door, trying to get a better view, tearing so hard to see the top of the bed that he ripped off a fingernail. His effort was so intense that only when he paused for breath did he notice the fine line of blood running down to his wrist. Then he felt the throbbing at the top of his finger. He eased the finger into his mouth to warm and soothe, then crawled to his pallet and cried. The firelight flickered and died down, but the man stayed, snoring loudly.

A narrow shaft of light came through the crack Bird had forced in the door and streaked across his sister's face. She was coughing as usual, a pecking cough from her shallow chest. Through the night, Bird listened for sounds from the other room, listened until the snoring stopped and boots scraped across the floor and stomped across the porch, down the steps, into the night. Bird's body tightened with each step. When the front door slammed, he sat up and watched his sister's face in the light as she gasped for breath. The light on her face disappeared. as their mother had moved to the door, blocking the light.

–You hush that crying, Bird, she said through the door. And mind your own business. You eating good, ain't you?

–Yea, we eating fine, Momma, but I don't feel right about what you doing.

–Ain't your place to feel right about it. Now hush your whining.

–Ain't just that, he said. Things is leaving me, Momma. Clarissa's face and Mr. Vickers's legs, and... The twine that secured the door zinged as it was unwrapped from the nail.

Generations

Carrying a kerosene lantern, his mother came into the room and knelt over Clarissa, who breathed with a steady rasp.

—Your sister ain't gone yet, poor child. What you talking 'bout Mr. Vickers?

Bird told her about the pants on the floor and how it seemed the man's legs had been jerked away when he hopped on the bed.

—That old goat ain't lost no legs, she said. Blowing out the light, she moved to Bird's pallet. How old you now, boy?

—Eleven.

—Clarissa's three, and Walter's seven, she said proudly. Y'all all so hard to do for, yet I loves you all. I ain't a dumb nigger, Bird. Dumb niggers don't live. I has to be a certain way with a white man like Mr. Vickers, a man who thinks God was talking to him when he give man dominion over the birds, and fish, and cattle, and ever creeping thing that creepeth upon the earth.

—He ain't gonna have dominion over me.

—Do you know what the word means, child?

—I seen it tonight.

—He ain't gonna have it over me no more neither. I ain't gonna ruin my health having a Vickers's child. I ain't the type can care for a brood of younguns. You heard me tell him, No. Told him I'd figured out about making babies, and when's safe if you don't want no more. He laughed and said they's room enough on his farm for one more nigger.

—How you gonna stop him?

—Tell him I done caught something from a city nigger passing through.

—Huh?

—Don't huh me, boy. How come I give you Bird for a name? Give it cause I 'spected you to be smart, and you are. But you know what the smartest bird is?

—Hawk?

–Naw. Always circling and showing his pretty self. Everybody know him. It's the mockingbird will fool you, pretending to be something he ain't. He ain't scared to sing at night. Only you don't necessarily know it's him, or whether he's being some other bird.

–You leaving, Momma?

She pulled Bird up with her as she stood.

–I'm getting on to being a man, he said. I can work even harder. We can get on without Mr. Vickers's help.

–Be hard times, she frowned, but we can talk about it.

He grinned and walked into the room heavy with the odor of the white man.

Within days the hard times came. Falling out of favor with Mr. Vickers, Florence was moved into the room with her three children to make room for Jab Moore, a tenant with a wife and six children. The first time Bird saw Belle, a high-yellow woman with round dark eyes, high cheekbones, a laugh full of even white teeth, body pliant as leather, he knew the cabin hadn't felt the last of Mr. Vickers.

Twelve people lived in the two-room cabin, and Bird's mother felt the crowding. By nature she required a modest amount of solitude, and it hadn't been that long ago when she had been a child herself and free to roam the woods, barefooted and unafraid, eating blackberries and drinking from the creeks. She had eaten better then.

Mr. Vickers cut their rations and brought her piles of sewing to do for his family. Florence was incompatible with the tedium. Clarissa got thinner on the diet of grits in the morning and greens at night. The tenant farmer and his family ate good meat three and four times a week courtesy of Mr. Vickers, who put Jab to riding a horse around the property at night to keep the

Generations

tenants from stealing, while he stole into Florence's old room for bed crashing with Belle. Something in Bird's heart would go hard and cold when he heard those boots on the steps. Each tread registered deep in Bird's gut.

Clarissa's coughing, the hunger, the nocturnal noises in the next room kept Florence awake nights and sent her wearily through listless days in the tight room. There seemed neither time nor inclination for her to move out into the healing sunlight.

To cheer up the place, Bird gathered the first wild roses and put them in a jar on the windowsill.

–You getting thin, Momma, and you don't laugh no more. We can't go on like this.

–We can, child. We could go on like this forever if we had to.

–What you mean? We ain't eating enough, sleeping enough. We're barely living.

–Mockingbird's scared of nothing. Got legs as thin as straw cause his wings'll take him anywhere. A mockingbird gives you hope. Gonna be one sings for us, child. I believes it.

Late that night, Bird was awakened by Mr. Vickers's roaring voice in the next room.

–Don't you get ungrateful on me, he yelled, like some of the other niggers.

Belle's children were crying.

–That woman ain't yours, Bird shouted. You leave her alone.

Bootsteps approached the door separating the two rooms.

The point of a knife thrust between the door and the doorjamb and sliced cleanly through the heavy twine. Mr. Vickers pushed the door open with force enough to knock a wasp nest loose from the wall. His dark hair clung to his forehead, and his shirt was open, exposing redness from belly button to head. On his chest were the faint imprints of a woman's hands with fingers spread wide.

Florence clasped her hand over Bird's mouth.

–Your pickaninny say that? Mr. Vickers asked, waving the knife at Florence. You're too late with covering that sass. He bent over, and Bird looked at the lines in the face, at the curved, yellow teeth. What do they call you, boy?

Florence took her hand back slightly, but held it ready like a harmonica player.

–Bird, he answered softly.

–Buzzard's more like it, Mr. Vickers bellowed. A black, stinking buzzard that eats the work of others. Want to eat this? He shoved the flat of the blade against Bird's cheek.

The boy dug his hand into his mother's shoulder.

–You get nosy with me again and I'll cut off that ugly nose of yours. You stick it in my business again, and you won't get it back.

Bird looked into the burning eyes, then fixed his vision on the fallen wasp nest. He stared at it for hours, stared until the room had emptied of the white man, though not of his odor.

Bird's mother sat on the floor and put her arms around her son.

–Anybody calls you a buzzard or a nigger or any name they think is stinking bad is worse than the name he calls you, is worse than what he imagines the name to be. Mister Vickers, she said softly, is worse than nigger, worse than buzzard.

Bird tried to be unafraid, but sometimes he woke in the night and felt to see if his nose was still there. Belle's children had their own fears. One day the oldest boy ran around the yard playfully beating the other children with a stick. Quit it, Mr. Vickers, they yelled. Oh, please don't beat me no more.

Generations

Getting caught in the spirit, Bird took the twine that Mr. Vickers had cut, and tied a mule shoe to each foot. He jumped up the steps, one loud stomp at a time. Pulling a round, flat pebble out of his pocket, he checked it as though it were a watch.

–Well, Belle, he said grandly, though not loudly enough for her to hear, I reckon's you and me's got time to get on with one 'fore that nigger of yours comes home. Now helps me outta these fine boots, but don't touch 'em with your nigger hands. From the yard came the applause of the other children.

That was Sunday play. During the week it was work in the woods. As a growing rail system pushed its line through the forest above the swamp, there was work for all Alwin Vickers's tenants. While Ella, the Vickers's cook, looked after Walter and Clarissa, Florence was sent out in the morning and afternoon driving a wagon with water barrels for the farm workers and the railroad crew. Bird and other young blacks became the cushioning crew, cutting saplings and piling them on the ground to absorb the shock of the giant pines and oaks that the large-muscled blacks felled with crosscut saws and broad axes. Using sledgehammers and wedges, the workers pried a block from the trunk, then did the finish trimming with the broadax. The work was hot and strenuous, and often no air at all stirred in the low forest. The men were paid fifteen cents for each cross tie, which Mr. Vickers, in turn, sold for thirty cents to a railroad foreman.

–This working night and day is testing my bones, Jab said to Bird when they were some distance from the others. You know why he's got me working nights?

Bird looked away.

–How come God to let somebody like that live and prosper? Bird asked.

–Ain't God's doing. Him and the Devil divvied the world long ago. Mr. Vickers was the Devil's draw. Jab leaned closer to

Bird. Don't you tell nobody, but I've got me a way at a gun. If ever I catch him with my woman.

–Let me see the gun, Bird said excitedly.

–Ain't got it. Says I got a way at one. They keeps it locked up over at the railroad office. Both looked at the shack across the swamp as though it were a shrine.

–Don't be no dumb nigger, Bird said. You'd be dead as fast as him.

The coming railroad also brought new black faces to the farm, the gandy dancers. One, a big round man with skin smooth and dark like strong coffee, quickly developed an interest in Florence and became a regular visitor to her room. He brought dressed chicken or rabbit, eggs and peaches. Every time he came, he brought food.

–Is that why they call him Tub, Clarissa asked one day. Even she was looking healthier.

–No, Bird laughed. Calls him that 'cause he's so fat.

–You chillun hush up about that man, Florence smiled. Calls him Tub 'cause he's full of love.

–Full of blubber, Walter said.

Lots of times when Tub was there, the door between the two rooms was left open, and everybody visited. The children would gather at his feet, and he was always willing to oblige with stories.

–See that, he'd say and pull back a lip to show a line of white teeth. Ain't got a tooth in my mouth.

–What's them then? Walter would ask.

–Diamonds. I was born with a mouth full of diamonds. Had a smart mammy though and she painted them white so's the white men couldn't catch the sparkle. White man would climb right in my mouth if he knowed it was full of diamonds.

–Would Mr. Vickers climb in there?

Generations

    –He'd have to take off them shining boots first so he wouldn't get nigger spit on them. Now this is the truth. He had them boots special made for him in Savannah by a German cobbler. I seen the shop myself when I was working the ships. I seen a lot of things. They take that pine sap what runs all over this farm and makes it into pitch, works it into the sides of ships to make 'em shed water.
    –Tell us about the time you went across the ocean, Walter said.
    Florence smiled. Tell us that again.
    –First I want to tell something for all these chillun here. They's gonna come a day when the city land and the farmland in this country is for blacks to own, too, so they pride and prosper same's a white. That day's a coming shore as I'm fat. He rubbed his thighs and watched the widening smiles all around him.
    –Now 'bout the ocean. I went across it one time when I wasn't much more than a boy. There's a piece of land out in there somewhere where it don't matter if a man's a nigger or not. I seen a white woman one day with a white man's arm around her waist, and the next day with a nigger's. Didn't make no mind to her. Long's she could eat olives and laugh.
    –What did her waist feel like? Florence asked.
    –I didn't say the nigger was me, Tub laughed.
    She smiled. Didn't say it wasn't neither.
    Tub's visits and being out in the air, rocking, with the swag of harness and jostle of water in the wooden barrels made Florence feel young and free again. The bed of the wagon was dark with spilled water and always cool. When there was time to spare, she'd pull behind a stand of trees and lie down in the back of the wagon, chewing the astringent pine needles and resting her head against the damp barrels. Like a seedling nestled in sunlight and moisture, she drew sustenance. Her legs grew springy and excited, and her spirit, light like air. And the workers, the

dark, sturdy enduring black men, smiled and laughed when she pulled into the shade, and they dropped their axes where they were, unless to ripple their muscles and sink the blade deep for the gleam of her approval.

Throwing the reins to the first man beside her, she'd straddle the seat, then walk to the back of the wagon, where she'd hand down a dripping gourd from each barrel. The hastily turned gourds sent water streaming down grateful chins and chests. From side to side she'd turn, dipping from one barrel then the other, a constant writhing dance, short in movement, long in effect. Some men sat on stumps and watched as though a traveling show had come to the very edge of the dark swamp, bringing a tall, dark woman to dance enchantment on a mobile stage.

Florence felt it, too, felt how strong the men were. Ill-fed, they could fell great trees; underpaid, they were rich with laughter. The glint of pine needles in the sun, the strong smell of pine, and her reflection rippling in dance on the water while a mockingbird sang from an ax-bitten tree gave her a sense of power she had never known. As long as the mules were hitched and the land unfenced there would be hope.

When Bird came for his turn, she dropped half a handful of sugar from her pocket into the gourd so deftly that only the broad smile of her son told what was done.

—Why you so happy today, Momma?

—Bird, she whispered, you old enough to take care of yourself, ain't you?

—Naw, Momma.

—Well, child, I done had a man asked me to marry, and I always wanted to be married.

—That don't change us none, does it?

Generations

—The man what I'm talking about feels you big enough, and he don't want you to be no burden to him. He's done said he'd be good to Walt and little Clarissa.
—Tub done said that.
—Yes.
—When you going?
—Tonight. 'Fore Mr. Vickers comes to Belle. So there won't be no trouble. She leaned over and kissed his hair. Don't you hear the mockingbird, child? Don't you hear it?

He heard the steady beat of hoofs as Mr. Vickers and his two sons, Tally, the oldest, and Robert, fourteen and big but shy, rode into the clearing. Mr. Vickers and Tally wore pistols in chest holsters. In the narrow sunlight, Mr. Vickers's boots glowed with a fresh polishing of tallow.

Leaning forward in the saddle, he spit at Jab's feet.
—You ain't doing neither one of us no good like that, he said, then turned to Tally. Look at him asleep with that nigger hat over his face. It happens every time. You feed a nigger good and he goes to sleep on you.

Jab turned his red eyes toward Mr. Vickers and scowled, but Mr. Vickers had already turned to the others.
—You niggers done had time to drink half the water in this county, he said. Let's get rolling 'fore it gets hard dark. He looked at Florence and the boy. That means you, too, Buzzard.

Like bullfrogs hearing threatening sounds, the workers hopped off the logs and moved into the shadows. The Vickers sat listening to the thuds of axes, the rasping of crosscut saws, and the long creaking of falling trees; the three white men sat immobile as the workers glistened with sweat in the underbrush.
—Look at her, Mr. Vickers said in a low voice to Tally. Must have got over that nigger sickness. She's looking plump and healthy again.
—Had them around her like a bitch in heat, Tally laughed.

Mockingbird

Hoping to see his mother before she left with Tub and the children, Bird hurried home through the darkness. When he got near the yard, he heard that sound he hated. But this time there was more than one man. There were several laughing and talking loud. He ran faster.

A new Model T was parked by the front porch. Bird watched Jab lead his wife and children quietly from their room, on past the outhouse and into the woods. The laughter had not come from their quarters.

Moving closer, he heard Clarissa's hollow cough and that eerie cry of Walter's, muffled as though he was afraid of being heard.

–Get away from me, Florence screamed. I done told you to get away.

Tally held Florence down on the bed while Mr. Vickers lowered Robert's pants. The boy stared dumbly at the wall as though in shock. Moving Robert aside, Mr. Vickers pushed Florence's dress up to her neck, then jerked Robert forward. He kneed him in the butt, causing the boy to fall on top. Clarissa tried to crawl on the bed with her mother, but Mr. Vickers brushed her aside with his boot, then grabbed Florence's heels. He pulled up on the heels while Tally pulled up on the shoulders in a coordinated, rhythmic motion as though tossing the white boy on a black blanket. The two men shook with effort and laughter while the boy gulped and gasped for air, his eyes closed and his red face pressed against the black breasts.

–I'm sorry, Florence, Robert groaned.

His father kicked him in the leg. A streak of tallow spread out on Robert's flesh.

–Don't you never apologize to a nigger bitch, Alwin Vickers bellowed, his face reddening. That's why you can't get hard.

Generations

    –Look, Daddy, Tally laughed. His whacker's getting littler.

    Watching from the window, Bird was transformed with anger. He could feel nothing but his head. It ached. It contained more than the design called for. He felt like a cannonball: put him in the room, and he would feed on his own flame, feed and explode and splinter the sorry scene.

    He did not know how he got in the room, but there he was kicking into the V of Mr. Vickers's stance, then he was on Robert, choking him, separating the two naked, sweaty bodies.

    –Goddamn Buzzard, Mr. Vickers muttered and reached for his pistol. He drew the gun and waited for an opening on the crowded bed.

    Letting go of Florence, Tally sprung to his father and blocked the view.

    –No, he said. Railroad crew's still around, Jab and all that bunch would know. You can't get by with it this time.

    –These woods have seen dead niggers before, Mr. Vickers said.

    –This ain't the time, Tally insisted.

    Bird stared at them all as they left, but not one of the Vickers looked at him. They were quick to the car and quickly gone. Clarissa put her arms around Bird. Walter sat in the corner, lost in high steady wail. Florence took the lye soap and water pitcher and walked outside.

    She was trembling even harder when she returned. Already one eye was puffy.

    –What happened to Tub? Bird asked.

    –He's coming, Florence said. Wanted to leave late so they wouldn't be no trouble. Tub was afraid Mr. Vickers wouldn't let us leave.

    –Let you leave? The war was over fifty years ago. Ain't been no slaves in all that time.

    –They ain't?

Mockingbird

—I'm gonna see that man dead, Bird said.
—You coming with us.
—Naw.
—You coming with us, she said again. I ain't gonna let you stay here so that man can kill you.
—I'll ride part of the way with you, Bird was saying by the time Tub arrived with his wagon and team of mules.

Crying and going off to get married, Florence sat on the seat beside Tub, with Clarissa and Walter fighting for possession of her other side. Bird rode in the back of the wagon, hanging his thin legs out and feeling his feet drag over the top of sandspurs and undergrowth.

—Why don't you do something about it, Tub, he asked.
—The man's too white, Tub said. You can come to Savannah with us. You can make us some good money loading ships. And you'll see the biggest shiniest water you ever laid eyes on. Same water our people come over when we was stole out of Africa.
—I ain't going nowhere, Bird said. My business is here.

He listened to the whisperings of his mother and Tub: Tie him? Find his way back sometime. What'll we do? Get him away he might forget. Ain't the type to forget such as that. Let him go then, uh? Let him go.

Florence stepped over the seat and sat beside him, pulling her knees to her chin and putting one arm around his shoulder. Don't you be no dumb nigger, she said. Whatever you do, don't be that. They rode on, bumping a little, while the wheels creaked, and the mules snorted in the quiet night.

When the mules reached the incline that led up to the highway, Bird slipped from his mother's arm and dropped to the ground.

—You take care, boy, Tub said, then urged the team forward. Bird stood in the sand until the sound of the wagon was gone, then after a look at the bright stars in the clear heaven, he

Generations

lowered his head and walked back along the wagon rut. He had had nothing to eat since morning, and his stomach hurt as though it had been hit with a big fist. The few berries left along the road were dry and dust-covered.

When he got to the cabin, Jab Moore and his family still had not returned, and his old room, lit by the moon, was empty and oppressive. The only thing he found that resembled food was the wasp nest that Mr. Vickers had knocked to the floor several weeks before. Two adult wasps lay dead beside the nest. Bird pinched the stingers off, then put the light wasps into his mouth. They were dry and hard. He held them against the inside of a cheek until they were soft, then he chewed them slow.

–White folks ain't the only ones can take, Bird said to himself. We got hands, too.

He walked through the woods, skirting the edge of the swamp where the ties had been cut. The leaves in the scrap piles were brown and curled, and stacks of ties cured on the high ground. The swamp water was unstirred. Saturday night had brought peace to the railroad construction across the swamp. All was so peaceful that Bird grew suspicious and afraid. Suddenly all the farm seemed coiled and cool, like a snake. But he walked on. He had his business.

He moved on toward the railroad office, cutting through a patch of rattling dry beans. The earth moved beneath his feet. It was more than the physical property of sand, which shifts when disturbed, it was more like something under the sand moving, sliding him along, converging everything toward a moment to be fixed in time.

By the time he neared the Vickers' place, a shotgun riding jauntily across his shoulder, Bird felt as though God was leading him. He made for the cooking shed, a long open building with a

Mockingbird

tin roof and brick oven with a vat at one end for cooking cane juice and a barbecue pit at the other. The moonlight and an erratic jump of flame from the coals were light enough to show Ella's hands folded in her lap, and her head, with mouth open, tilted back in the chair. A butcher knife lay on a nearby table.

The rich odor of the slowly cooking meat spread out in a circle that Bird was all too willing to penetrate. Unthinkingly, he moved steadily toward the target. Cats, awaiting a feast, scurried at his approach.

Two spits loaded with goat meat sizzled over the coals. Finding a croker sack behind the chair and using a rag to protect his hands, Bird emptied one spit into the sack. With the shotgun in one hand and the heavy sack dragging from the other, he lurched from the shed.

He didn't stop until he reached a log cabin a half mile away. It was on a new place that Mr. Vickers had bought and was the last standing slave quarters in the area. The cabin leaned forward on crumbling sills, but the fireplace stood solid, and the roof was mostly intact.

Inside by the fireplace, Bird emptied the croker sack and relished the two legs and section of rib. He attacked the ribs first, slicing with the knife, then cramming his mouth full, slicing, then cramming. He laid the bones aside carefully for later gnawing.

The meat was perfect, juicy and tender. Time had been right for the spit to come off. Time was right for the other, too, but Ella slept on.

Having but one window, the cabin was fairly dark, even with the full moon. Bird worked his way into the first leg before he was satisfied. It wasn't until his hunger was sated that he thought again of Mr. Vickers, wished the goat were the man being sliced bit by bit. *Yea*, Bird thought, licking the grease from his fingers, *I got me some business with that man.*

Generations

    Bird put the remaining meat back in the croker sack and stuffed it up the chimney until it wedged tight. Then he walked to the window and looked out at the moon shining through the piney woods. The opening had never had panes. He straddled it as though a horse, hanging one leg out in the bright night while the other scraped the dirt floor of the cabin. He tied the rag around his chest, much like Mr. Vickers's chest holster. Hey, Buzzard, he shouted. Don't you get ungrateful on me like some of the other niggers. I gonna cut off your fat, ugly nose, gonna slice your ribs till they lean, Bird laughed, daring in his play. Hey I's gonna get you even if you goes to sleep. Bird spit against a pine trunk. You know how it is. Happens ever time. You feed a nigger good, and he goes to sleep on you. *Yea, Yea, Yea, he sleeps good, white man. But he wakes good, too.*

    Bird woke in the foggy gray of predawn and thought of his family. He wondered if Clarissa was coughing, if his Momma had stopped crying, if they had all got to Savannah. How many farms over would that city be, he wondered. Tub had said it took a smart of days to get there by wagon. Bird knew they'd be proud to see him now, see all the food he had. He was doing okay by himself.

    Bird retrieved the sack, threw it over his shoulder, and crawled out through the window. There was enough left to give a leg to Jab. He had a lot of children to feed.

    The fog had burned off by the time the Model T pulled hurriedly in front of the old slave quarters. Tally ran behind the car and pointed to where a sack had left a deep trail across the sandy road.

    –Bet he's inside, Mr. Vickers said. Come on, Robert, let's get him.

    –I don't feel like it, Pa, the boy said, holding his head in his hands. I don't feel so good.

Mockingbird

—Come on, I said. I ain't asking. Last night I showed you what a nigger woman is good for. This morning I aim to show you what's good for a thieving nigger.

Robert's health improved when he saw the cabin was empty. Tally sniffed out the cache in the chimney, while Mr. Vickers found footsteps leading down through the woods.

—Heading to Jab's, Mr. Vickers said.

—Is it Jab? Tally asked.

—Nope. This one ain't full grown, but he's gonna wish he was full dead.

—Damn it, Bird, Jab yelled. You get on away from here. Word done floating the Vickers is looking for you. What you doing here? Why didn't you stay with Tub and your momma?

—I brought you some food, Bird said, standing proudly on the porch.

—I'm hungry as the day I was born, Jab said, taking a step nearer the sack, but I'd rather not be seeing food or you right now. You gone git me in trouble, Bird. You get rid of that gun and get shut of that knife. The man's gonna kill you good, Jab said, envious of the boy's boldness.

—Don't you want to look at the roasted meat I brought?

—Meat's good, Jab said, putting his nose to the sack. Fine good. But it ain't good you here, he said, drawing back.

—I can get us something like this every night, Bird was saying proudly as the Model T pulled up to the cabin.

—Run, dump this sack in the outhouse, Jab whispered to his oldest daughter. Don't let them see you. Hurry.

Bird leaned against the cabin's door frame. From the outside, his left arm was visible, his right hidden by the wall.

Jab turned to the approaching men.

—What I can do for you gentlemen? he asked.

Generations

    –Looking for a goat, Mr. Vickers said and planted a shiny boot on the bottom step.
    Bird cringed at the heavy sound. Tally waited by the car.
    –Ain't seen no goat, Jab said.
    Tally moved toward the porch.
    –Don't mind if we look around do you?
    –You can look around outside all's you want, Jab said.
    –What's wrong with inside? Mr. Vickers asked, pulling out his watch and checking the time. He had on Sunday clothes with a clean white shirt and thin black tie. The holster's bulge was visible under his coat.
    –Don't want you or your boys inside my place, Jab said.
    –You getting mighty sassy. How long you been owning this place? I don't 'member no deed or no money. You ain't never had nothing in your life without me giving it to you. And you don't seem to appreciate none of it. That's how come I quit loading your family with vittles, and that's how come I want to see if you're stealing from me like the rest of 'em.
    –Don't want you inside, Jab said, raising his voice.
    –Ain't your place, nigger, Mr. Vickers said calmly. All this is mine. He brought his other leg to the bottom step. Robert moved reluctantly out of the car. He glanced at Belle. She looked terrified.
    Y'all ain't all coming in here now, Mr. Vickers. You listen to me, Jab insisted. He motioned for Bird to give him the shotgun, but the boy didn't see him. He was staring at the boots.
    –Ain't no telling what we might do, is there Jab? Mr. Vickers said, and a foot moved up to the next step.
    In one smooth motion, Bird leaned, clearing his right side, and fired a load of buckshot into the leg that wouldn't quit coming.
    Mr. Vickers was blown from the steps, his leg from his body. He seemed to totter a moment on the one leg, then collapsed a

length away from the other. The children screamed and gathered around Belle.

Robert and Tally, pale and shaking, dragged their father to the car. They piled him in the front seat.

–You nigger bastard, Tally yelled.

Tally drove off as Robert ran back for the leg. With the limb on his shoulder, Robert twirled around and around. His eyes stretched wide. He kicked the sand, all the time emitting a muffled cry as though his mouth wouldn't open. All that came out was a short, repetitive grunt. Then as though the gears of his body finally meshed, Robert ran through the field and by the white oak, taking the shortcut home, holding the surprisingly heavy leg by the shin, the tallow rank at close quarters and the thong double-knotted with a neat bow, which flapped like twin nooses.

Bird watched Robert until the torn, red pulp was out of sight, then he rushed down into the yard and jumped from blood spot to blood spot. He held his foot behind him, making himself appear legless from the knee down. He hopped and shrieked (though Mr. Vickers had done neither), throwing back his head and shouting, Oh, Lord, I is got. Don't let the Buzzard get me, keep me from the Buzzard.

A child of six found the dance enthralling and slowly joined in. Seeing this, Bird regained his balance and ran to the woodpile. He returned with a leg-sized log of pine over his shoulder and moaned and twirled and twirled in widening circles until he fell dizzy to the ground beside the child, who had been unable to perfect the one-legged dance. Bird pretended to attach the log to the knee of the little boy by placing it against the kneecap and pouring sand over the junction. The sand slid smoothly from his hands and spread across the boy's pants. He was adding more when the log was kicked across the yard. Bird looked up into Jab's eyes. You better get, too, boy, he said to Bird.

Generations

Jab walked down the road to the left, away from the route Tally Vickers had driven.

—Where's daddy going? the boy asked, then ran down the road after him. Daddy, he called.

Bird sat in the yard. The log had rolled through a puddle of blood and had added a layer of gritty sand. All the birds had flown deep into the woods at the shot, but one had returned. White and gray, flicking his tail from side to side, he looked about and began his song.

Inside the cabin, the old man spoke softly. I told you not to hear no mockingbird on me, Momma. I told you.

Florence didn't hear. She didn't move as Bird closed her eyes, eyes that had been unseeing even before death.

Bird walked out of the house toward the white oak. They had all gone and left him now. Clarissa, who had never been meant to live long in this world, Tub long gone, Walter gone to Spain and never heard from.

—She's gone, Robert, Bird said as he neared the tree. He looked up disdainfully at the mockingbird before sitting beside Robert.

—She's gone, Robert echoed. He rubbed his face with a callused hand and looked at Bird. You ever forgive me for your momma?

—It wasn't you who done it, Bird said, once more seeing Tally and Alwin Vickers pinning his mother on the bed, and Robert's contorted face pressed against the breasts. You didn't do nothing, did you?

—I couldn't. Physically, morally, emotionally. Name it, I couldn't. I never was like my old man or Tally. I didn't know till last year that it was you, not Jab, killed Daddy. Tally slapped me years ago when I said I'd always admired Jab for being able to do

Mockingbird

what I had dreamed of. But I was sorry about what they did to Jab.

–I'm the one should be sorry for that.

–They would have got him anyway. Had they caught you when they did Jab, had they had you both together, they wouldn't have believed you fired the shot. You could of told them a hundred times and they wouldn't have believed it.

–You *admire* me for killing your daddy?

– Ma always said Daddy was born mean and went bad. He looked at Bird. All that seems long ago.

–Don't feel it to me.

The branches in the treetop shook gently as the bird launched.

Bird was glad to see him gone.

–I'm sorry about your Ma, Robert said. You know she didn't want this fence. Yelled at me when she heard me putting it up. Couldn't stand fences, but loved mockingbirds. Why you reckon she loved them so much?

–Damn if I know.

The mockingbird gained altitude with that slow flight pattern of wing beats, each wing sporting a long white streak, its black legs tucked tightly, its body boldly gray.

If She Should Die

–There's only the slow way, he had said.
 –The fast.
 –You've always been impetuous. Tell you about the slow. It's conservative, but it's generally more effective.
 –The fast.
 –Now, Carla, not many of my patients got better by swallowing a whole bottle of medicine at one time.
 –I don't want two teaspoons four times a day for the rest of my life.
 –Slow doesn't mean for the rest of your life.
 –Mix me up a big bottle.
 –My God, girl, sounds like nothing's wrong. Sounds like you're ready to take on the world.
 –Talking brave is easy.
 Her grandfather's old voice cracking over the phone had convinced her. It was not what had been said or how it had been said, but the voice itself, the disembodied conveyor of memories and hope that had made her want to visit, made her believe a cure was possible. She held to that resolve in spite of the solicitudes of her attentive friends, who escorted her on the drive from Atlanta.
 –Would you like the window up or down?
 –Why don't you ride up front?

Generations

–Are you hungry?
–Would you like me to move over and give you room to stretch out?
–You people are driving me crazy, Carla said.
–Don't say that, they urged, then grew silent.

The highway passed through a vast pine and hardwood forest with only a few houses, some deserted, etched into the trees. Forest had reclaimed forgotten cotton fields and grew through roofless houses with faded whitewashed fronts. At post-sunset gloom, Carla saw a light in a distant fire tower and wondered what it would be like to be in the cabin high above treetop in such a desolate land. There had been a time when she would have found out, would have climbed flight after flight of metal steps, but now even the thought of height made her cringe.

–Roll up the window. Carla's cold.
–I'm not, she protested as the glass rose into the felt liner.
–I, for one, have never heard of getting goose bumps from being too warm.

Carla hated being afraid. Fear was insidious and unpredictable. A curtain blew in her apartment, and her heart beat wildly, her mind forming from mere wind the hardy substance of an intruder. Her telephone rang—a death in the family. The doorbell chimed—three hooded rapists crouched and waited.

Her head hurt; she felt sick. She reached over and rolled the window down halfway and took a deep breath.

–I think it will do you good to get out of Atlanta for the weekend.

It puzzled her—was *it* something that had already happened, was about to happen, or something that would never happen? The more *it* hovered at some edge of her consciousness, the greater her irritation and fright.

–You should have a good time at your grandfather's farm.
–Fresh air and good food, just what the...

Carla closed her mind to the voices that made it sound like she was a little girl in a storybook, running through pastures of bluets and spring beauties with ducks waddling after her and a white dove perched on her shoulder. The visit would not be idyllic; she hadn't time for that. She had her plans. She had a path to follow, a century-old one from her grandfather's house to an abandoned mill beside Panther Creek. As a boy, her grandfather had ridden to the mill once a week during late summer and autumn to spend the night and be ready for Saturday's early grinding. Thirteen miles, then a night alone at a time when there were still panthers in the land; big cats with stark yellow eyes had perhaps prowled through the mill while he slept.

Carla would retrace his journey and, in the process, cast off her large, impenetrable fears of darkness and solitude and leave them to rot like carcasses in the forest. In the place of her sloughed-off fears, she hoped to fill the gaps in her mind, psyche, and gut with calm, hope, understanding, and acceptance.

The interstate traffic seemed variegated night bugs to Carla. Some elongated, others squat, but all noisy and hasty, spinning their rubber legs along a long cut healed with cement. Their most notable feature a pair of hard, round eyes that beamed whitish-yellow light. The bugs were uncaring, oblivious, incessant. They would go on and on. Five years from now, fifty years, five hundred, some human kind would stand on the dark hills above the interstate and watch the steady metallic beat of greedy cells.

Margy pulled up the ramp into the glare of the exchange; she drove past the golden arch, Pizza Hut, Burger King, predictable clones, and onto the cement apron leading to the pumps of the Chevron station. As Margy filled the gas tank, Carla watched the customers in the beverage section. The one

Generations

with two cases of Budweiser caught her attention. He wore a dirty cap with a Ford emblem. One eye was set a little higher than the other in a puffy, red face with a double row of yellow teeth. One front tooth was missing. The absence showed when he laughed, and he laughed a lot as he talked with the young clerk, who looked as though she couldn't wait for him to leave.

A scar, curved like a mountain highway, ran from eye to lip above the tooth gap. His shirt was unbuttoned, revealing a smooth, fat, sunburned upper torso sown with a thick cover crop of curly black hair.

–Wouldn't you hate to meet that in the dark? Margy whispered.

Another friend looked at Carla's pale skin and the dark worry arcs under her eyes. *Twenty-five should be an age of joy*, the friend thought.

–Let's don't talk so much, she said. Carla needs her rest.

Carla didn't hear her. *I want to conquer it myself*, Carla thought. *I'm going to face my fear. I want to know what it smells like, tastes like, what it wants. I don't want to fight or run, but to find it, real or imagined, substance or fabrication, find it and stare it down until it shrivels.*

The farm was located in the hills ninety miles north of the interstate. The closer they got, the narrower the road, the denser the vegetation. Tree limbs intertwined overhead, creating a series of leafy tunnels. By the roadside, kudzu monopolized ditches and embankments; it dangled from tree to tree.

–A perfect place for an elves' picnic, someone said.

–I wouldn't live here, Margy said. Couldn't pay me to live here.

–Ah, but would you pay to be healed here or to die here? Carla murmured to herself, drawing the place once more into her imagination, the way a person struggling for breath might benefit by drawing a draft of cleaner, richer mountain air. She had always sought and sometimes found healing here in the woods, by the springhead, enclosed by the hillside springhouse, now tumbling in upon the boxed holding tanks of chestnut, with the exiting stream now carrying waterlogged splinters as well as clear cool water that poured from the springhouse in a foot-wide stream that ran through a course of watercress. She had sought and sometimes found healing up the far hill as well, in the six-gable, two-story house with three-quarters wrap-around porch, the white frame house set against a hillside under a canopy of shagbark hickory with clumps of jonquils, long past their annual bloom, set in scatters about the yard, with a large, airy kitchen that opened to a separate porch and beyond that small porch, barns and outbuildings and the scraggly descendants of what had once been a large and productive apple orchard. An old homestead forged in part from moments of years past and of hearts and minds and the flesh and longings of a few progenitors Carla had known, who came from hearts and minds of humans she had never known and could not, with accuracy, imagine. Beyond the broken unshapely trees rose the southern range of the Blue Ridge Mountains, parts still dense and isolated with flowing water named Moccasin Creek and Panther Creek and with mountains named Tray and Black Rock. *If only,* Carla thought, *it's really true that returning to certain places native to us, long part of us and our families, is like an elixir, a healing draught that enters us and gives our bodies strength and our minds ease.*

Behind the car, a distant light gained ground until it became the headlights of a trailing pickup truck, which pulled close enough to flood the interior with brightness. There was time and a long stretch of road for passing, but the truck kept its position. Margy crimped the rearview mirror upward and eased the pressure on the accelerator.

Generations

—What's following us? Carla asked. Then she knew. What pushed them on, what followed her was some segment of herself, something cut loose from her other, something once terrible inside her that now outside her and free terrorized her remaining self. Following her was something that had a life of its own and a mission to subdue and destroy her. It was the thing that rustled her curtain in Atlanta on windless days. She shook involuntarily.

Not until Margy flipped the turn signal near the farmhouse did the truck pass. Blasting his horn, the driver roared by.

How long, Carla wondered, *could an old house like this maintain its identity, how long did it have before housing developments sat like cow pies around it, how long would it have breathing room, how long could one old house shelter memories of generations of the same family?*

Everything gets smaller as you get older, Carla thought as she sat in the kitchen. On visits as a child, she had run around the table, had sprinted from refrigerator to sink as though the room were a gym. She had laughed in that room, cried there. Now, she sat with one hand clasping the other. Only in such a self-imposed cluster could she conceal the trembling.

—When you were eleven, you used to leave this kitchen in the night and ride alone across the mountains to the mill.

—That was a long time ago, Carla, her grandfather said.

—There are no panthers anymore.

—What we have now are worse than panthers. Vultures, I call them: punks perched in the backs of pickups parked along lonely roads. Drinking all night long. Watching for any excuse for devilment. You'd have to cross one of their favorite spots. Besides, you just got here. Can't you wait till tomorrow?

—Help me saddle a horse, she said. That's the big bottle I've been waiting for.

Her pronouncement was delivered bravely, but the courage was only surface deep. She dreaded the challenge she had set. She felt shaky, but she attributed part of it to fatigue and another part to the speedy drive from Atlanta.

–I'll talk you out of it yet, he said as they walked out of the kitchen and across the small porch.

–Did you ever take me to the mill? Did I ever ride along that trail with you?

–No, for some reason you've never gone that I know of. Not even when I was younger, and we used to take long trail rides.

–I think I've been, she said, stepping out into the darkness beyond the reach of kitchen light. Not all the way to the mill, but close. Tonight, maybe the memory will come back. Carla glanced at the sky. Have you noticed the moon is yellow like a stained tooth?

He shook his head and then was ashamed of the gesture that so openly and strongly expressed his doubts about her traveling alone. Whether she had been or not, was not, to his mind, the immediate problem. Her emotional state was.

Looking up at the same moon that had lighted his youthful trips to the mill, he walked across the yard. Carla's hands brushed his as he walked past her into the tack room.

As a child, Carla had felt that her grandfather was old but timeless. Now he was older; nothing was timeless. When he came out with the gear, he was panting, his cheeks hollow like two small cups. Carla wondered how much longer he would be able to take care of himself, feed his animals, cultivate his garden. She saw what her mother meant when she had said he wasn't thick enough to stop the wind. Carla wondered if he feared his future. She didn't ask. He remained silent.

As he worked with the leather, he breathed heavily. His head close to Blaze's head; Carla's close to his. Blaze, a sleek, black Morgan with large black eyes, white diamond on her forehead,

Generations

and white hair on her front legs from cannons to hoofs, wiggled her skin with excitement. As the horse moved closer, the man was reminded of how few people knew about horses anymore. Didn't know how to smooth a saddle blanket, cinch a girth strap; how few anymore strapped a curry comb to their hand and worked it across bristly hide.

–The trail is clear and certain, he said. Even at night, especially a full-moon one like this. A little past the halfway point, the path will open onto a road. Go left there and keep on till you're past the church. Make sure you're a half mile, not a mile, not a quarter, a half mile past the church before you cut back into the woods. You get the wrong trail there, and no one will find you.

Part of him wanted to drag her into the house and keep her from going, even though he knew physical constraint was impossible; the other part wanted her to try, even though he didn't give much for her chances. How would she feel if she had to rein the horse back in? What if she made it to the mill and back and every gait was terror? Nothing would be conquered either way. What would be vanquished instead would be part of her spirit. Too much had been going on in her mind. Too many fabricated fears. But there were real dangers as well: a wrong turn, a low limb, loose boulders, snakes out in the humid summer night, a spooked horse. The more he thought, the more he was certain of the outcome.

–Why such shame in being afraid? he asked as he tightened the girth.

He hadn't practiced medicine in twenty years but found himself straining to catch the timbre of her breathing, the movement of her pupils as he counted, with peripheral vision, the spurts of the artery in her slim neck.

–You've never been afraid. Steady doctor, steady father. Steady, steady.

If She Should Die

–I've been thinking since we talked on the phone.

–I know what you've been thinking, but I don't want to see another psychiatrist. I want to work it out myself.

–Your friends helped you up here. I'm willing to help. What's wrong with competent, professional help?

–The last one gave me a prescription: Valium twenty mg. They knock me out for days. Her take, in addition to a hundred dollars an hour: I'm running fast. Six colleges in four years. Temporary jobs since graduation. A weird, disjointed involvement with guys, up to a point. She said my only commitment is to my fear. Carla shrugged. Maybe she's right.

–Twenty milligrams? That's strong, Carla. The doctor must think you need to be knocked out for awhile.

–I don't want to find my courage or my death in a bottle of tranquilizers. I want to find it here. I think about myself too much, but in that thinking I've unleashed some strong fears. I'm scared of something that stays inside me smoldering like something buried deep in some compost pile of my memory. I'm scared of what it is, scared to dig and find it. I'm afraid of the dark and of death; I'm scared of being alone with what waits inside me.

–Those are things to fear at times, he said softly. Did you finish the prescription?

–Two down the hatch, the rest down the toilet.

You're in no shape for it, he thought as she settled into the saddle. Even in the dull light of the bare bulb hanging from a cord in the tack room, her new boots of Spanish leather gleamed. Her jeans, too, were new, as was a bright, flannel pullover, which she stuffed into a saddlebag. Her hair was cut short. It held tight and dark against her scalp as the worry circles held dark and tight under her eyes. Except for a look as of smeared charcoal under her eyes, her face was pale; her smile forced. Every inch of the outfit, every scent of its newness, every act of changing her

Generations

looks—the haircut, the long dangling earrings—spoke of how desperately hopeful her planning for this had been. *You need help*, he thought, but he didn't know how to convince her. Twenty milligrams of valium was enough to calm Blaze. Seeing Carla now, he wondered if she had flushed the pills down the toilet. He hoped she had.

–Try to talk to a young person these days, he muttered.

Instantly he was disgusted with both his thoughts and with what he had already said. Carla had enough swirling inside her; she didn't need the additional weight of his careless words or his unvoiced concern. And so he slapped her boot, an old gesture, an old superstition between them. Perhaps it was more than that. A wish, a prayer that the traveler undertake a safe and happy ride.

–Be alert, he said, be gentle with Blaze, and come back proud.

He stood, ran his hands up along the post, patted a saddle, and walked away, leaving it empty of everything except the temporary warmth of his hand. As he walked across the yard, he turned his jacket collar up against his thin neck. He walked slowly to the house. Standing on the porch, he watched Carla come back into view on the bald ridge above the barn. The horse worked steadily; the rider crouched in the saddle.

–Carla, he called in a voice barely strong enough to move his lips. *When I need a yell that will rustle leaves and stop Blaze in her tracks, I get this.* And then he laughed, though there was not much uproar there either as a tightness grew in his chest.

In the moonlight at the top of the hill, the horse hesitated. She pawed the earth and stamped hard with her rear hoofs, sending tremors through earth and rider, shock waves that assaulted Carla's fragile resolve. Her shoulders drooped, giving her the appearance of sitting short in the saddle as she looked back at the isolated farm. Pale moonlight pressed through the thin clouds and showed the dark outlines of forested ridges that spread like hairy fingers. The outbuildings looked sturdier in the flowing light of the full moon, their corrugated tin roofs bright like mountain streams. Inside one building, chickens roosted. Horses settled down after the disturbance in the barn. There was comfort in the aroma of new-mown hay and in the knowledge that this was the moment she could turn back. Her friends would never know she had given up, for she had never told them her plans. And her grandfather, probably already in bed, would be understanding and relieved. But she didn't have to live with them; she had to live with herself, with her opinion of herself. That was an irreversible lifetime union.

Taking a last look and a deep breath, Carla nudged the restive mare in the ribs and moved slowly down the hill, leaving the farm behind a ridge. Ahead lay a narrow trail through thick woods.

She felt a rhythm and a beauty in the canter of the horse through the night, a feeling of naturalness in the laboring of equine lungs and the slapping of leaves across face and arms. The naturalness is what Carla tried to hold to, the sense of horse-sway, the jostle of rough path. As long as she could do that, she thought she would be okay. She had been hurt more by what she had imagined to be than by what was. She'd keep her mind glued to reality, which was her riding alone, of her own volition, over a mountain trail.

Once her brother, he was three years old then, had thought he was alone in their backyard and lowered his pants to his knees to take a leak near some bushes when Scent, their father's cold-nosed bird-dog, nudged him in the rear. Her brother had arched his lower body so much to escape whatever had him, that his stream of urine rose straight up into the air and then

Generations

cascaded down upon his head. The family always laughed at that; remembering, Carla laughed, then was taken aback at the laughing echo. *Was that my voice?* she wondered.

Carla suddenly tensed. She had gotten away from feeling the ride and had wandered back into her mind, deep among the forebodings, the memories.

She shivered at the onslaught of a sudden nausea and a sweating dizziness. She tried to break away from the pattern of her thoughts. Action, not panic, is what she wanted. Leaning down against the horse's neck, she felt the equine muscles and warmth. Through a gap in the foliage, she saw the hillside across the cove. The far edge of the cove itself spread out, bright in the moonlight reaching up the distant hill and beyond that to a black sky banked with stars. *So natural, so beautiful,* she thought, trying to calm herself as her breathing grew more rapid. *So open.*

But what she felt was the constriction, the hand tightening on her wrist, the vise of the mountains sliding closer and closer, and the hoofs pounding as though the taut earth were a drum. Were fear an outfit of tight-fitting clothes, it could not have enveloped her more completely. Carla's muscles tightened. The runaway breathing brought lightness to her head. Her heart pounded the walls of her chest like a fist. And then as though she had been hammered by a limb, the lightness emptied from her skull, and a heavy ache moved across her forehead and up her temples.

–Quit it, she screamed, rubbing her temples, yet feeling the headache intensify. Quit thinking like this. There's nothing to be afraid of.

She had read that anger and anxiety could not coexist, that fear and forceful action were not compatible, yet after the rush of panic, she felt nothing but the sweat of her defeat and the depletion of her energy. She had no reserve for anger. All that was left was a deep feeling of shame.

If She Should Die

–Quit it, she yelled. Quit feeling this way. Quit thinking like this.

Her mind didn't obey her commands. The more she commanded, the more a part of her resisted, the dizzier she became. The hard ground seemed to ring under the hoofs. She had to hold on to the reins; she had to force herself to stay in the saddle. Oak roots crossed the trail like giant snakes, and the moon looked lost in the vast, silent sky.

Leaning forward in the saddle, she again rested her head against the mare's neck and closed her eyes. Time passed, miles passed, with the universal, honorable odor of horse lather, the deep breaths of rider. Comforted by the frothy sweat, the vibrant smell of horse, Carla rode in self-imposed darkness. Focusing on that comfort, Carla kept one hand against Blaze's flank and didn't flinch when a sharp, bare branch scratched her scalp. Through the contrived blindness, the obliviousness to possible danger, Carla stayed the panic. She opened her eyes when she heard the flow of a stream.

Dismounting, she took a seat by a whitewater pool and planned the next stage. She'd be more aggressive, less dependent. She had relied too much on the mare. Blaze was her security. All she had to do was turn the horse around, maintain enough consciousness to hang on, and Blaze would get her back to the farm. Maybe it would be better if she tied the horse by the stream and proceeded alone, really alone.

Carla dropped her hands into the clear water. No matter how far down she put them, they could be seen floating limp, white, and trembling. She swirled her hands and retested—fear stayed visible. She churned her hands in anger and stirred up a whirlpool. Whatever was left of her time was before her. She would live it, not fear it, and if she couldn't live it without fear, she would end it. *Probably fearfully,* she thought. She wanted calm; she demanded calm. One way or the other, she'd get it. If nothing else the vial of thirty-eight valiums she had in the pocket of her flannel shirt stuffed in the saddlebag would do the trick.

Carla remounted and guided Blaze with a tight rein as the trail neared the road. Ten slow yards. Stop. Listen. Ten more. Five times she repeated before she heard the voices. They sounded far away, and the direction couldn't be pinpointed. She'd have time to turn around if she so chose, for now she'd keep moving. As the elapsed yards increased, she knew the voices were up ahead. Yet she had the feeling, wild imaginative speculation, she told herself, that something was following her, too.

She guided Blaze up the hillside and waited for her pursuer to pass. She could hear the roadside voices to her right, but to her left the woods held silent. *In the mind,* she told herself finally, and led the horse to the trail, convinced that if she could keep her composure and ride into the road and then another half mile until the trail turned back into the woods beyond the clapboard Calvary Holiness Baptist Church, she could do almost anything.

A tall, skinny youth sitting on the hood of one of the trucks yelled, What's that? as Blaze trotted into the opening where the trail emptied into road.

Other youths, beer cans in hand, turned to look.

Taking a deep breath, Carla urged Blaze forward. In the full moon glow, she felt naked and knew they were all watching her. At a glance, she saw they had, for the moment, stopped drinking, paused in their routine by the unexpected. Then one, then two bodies moved toward her. Carla saw them dragging her from the horse, taking her into the culvert, laughing, saw it in her mind and reacted by kicking the horse and driving her fast down the road.

A can flew from the back of a truck. Flashing in the moonlight, it neared the long arms of the youth sitting on the hood. He caught it casually. There was an explosion of spray as the tab was pulled. Beer sloshed over the hood.

–Happy trails, someone yelled.

The man sitting behind the steering wheel smiled, winked his eye, and fanned with his Ford cap.

Carla's neck muscles ached from tension, her head throbbed, and her shoulders were scrunched up as though to hide her head as she rode hard.

Carla had mixed feelings when she neared the abandoned house that served as the final landmark—the mill a mile away down the left fork of the trail. A century ago, this had been a thriving dwelling in the middle of a large apple orchard. The apple trees now long rotted, their once orderly rows now dense with the irregular sprouting and growth of forest. This the cabin, older, not as steady, a leaning shack now overgrown with saplings, with part of its roof missing, its porch sunken to the ground. Casting a long shadow down the hill, the plain wooden structure sat soft and still in the moonlight.

Carla stared hard at the cabin and tried to take a deep breath. The last doctor she had suffered through a series of visits with had said that running, whether mental or physical, was almost always a defense, a way to protect. She said that memory could run away, too. It had to be coaxed, convinced to return.

–I've had enough of coaxing, personal and professional, Carla said. It's the big bottle I want.

Carla felt her lungs fill not with cool, sustaining oxygen but with hot, suffocating fear. It was as if something inside her, something below the surface of memory, had boiled for years. Now the turmoil organized into harsh, distinctive forms.

Generations

Her vision focused, memory blinked. She tried again to take a deep breath. Her mouth was pressed against flank just above the shoulder. Her breath stifled by the frothy sweat of a horse. She struggled. A hand against the back of her head held her down. The other part of her dangled from the right side of the horse's neck. Her pants were down. A large, smooth hand moved across her rump. She tried again to breathe. The hand on the back of her head lightened. From waist up, she hung upside down. With one eye, she saw the cabin, with the other the man in the saddle. He had a large, pocked nose, blue eyes rimmed with red, a clean-shaven chin.

Carla dropped her head and watched a black truck pull down a tree-bound rutted road near the cabin.

—Show time, the man said.

Carla could hear the sneer in his voice.

He sprang from the horse, jerked Carla by the arms. He dragged her across the horse's neck and mane and secured her across his shoulder.

Her pants fell down to her ankles.

The horse snorted, reared, hit the earth hard with its front hoofs then trotted off toward the truck.

Both of the man's hands were tight against Carla's rump. She heaved. What had been inside her flew threw the air and splattered against the cabin steps.

As though she were a load of firewood, he threw her toward a mattress beside the stone hearth.

Before she landed, she had reached for her pants.

—Leave 'em down, he said. Or I'll kill you.

From the sink he grabbed a glass and flung water across the room. It splattered against her hair and forehead.

—Clean up your mouth, he commanded.

A long, wooden table ran along the center of the tiny cabin's one room. Beer bottles lay scattered about the table. A tall bottle of whiskey sat in the table's center. The cabin smelled of beer and cigarettes. A tripod, aligned perfectly midpoint of the table, sat between the table and the cabin's one window. Mounted on the tripod was a heavy-looking, metal camera with two round sections. The camera was tilted.

He dropped his pants to his knees and laughed. Even with her eyes closed, she saw his hands on himself, saw his mouth open, saw his sneer.

–I don't like the way you're not looking at me, the man shouted.

But she was looking at him. With her eyes closed. With her brain saying NO NO NO NO, she could see little else but him, a tall, angular man with a pale, white body and the whitest, straightest teeth she had ever seen, capped off by a gold tooth in the center of the top row.

She would fight as best she could. What she wanted and needed most was to be strong, fearless, to unnerve him with her fighting resolve. That's what she wanted, that's what she prayed for, but she was the one unnerved, she the one whose entire body trembled and whose legs could not support her as she struggled to stand. Opening her eyes, she saw a woman, blonde and stocky with thick legs. The woman had on tight-fitting white shorts and was barefooted. She stood by the kitchen table.

–I came to stop you this time, the woman said.

–Shut up, the man yelled. You're stopping nothing. We agreed. You came to take pictures like always.

–I came to stop you.

–No, he said. You like filming me educating these girls.

–She's crying, the woman said. Don't you get tired of them crying?

–I haven't hurt her yet.

The woman picked up the whiskey bottle. She held it by the neck and took two steps toward the man.

Generations

–You gonna find it hard to drink it thataway, he mocked.

She came closer. Carla watched the bare feet moving deliberately, the toes pressing down firmly at the end of each stride. From across the room, Carla saw the man's body tense.

–You crazy, the man said. And if you keep walking toward me, if you keep looking at me thataway, you gonna be crazy dead.

The woman lunged and swung the whiskey bottle hard against the side of the man's head. Whiskey rushed from the bursting bottle and splattered about Carla; blood spurted, too, escaping from the man's skull.

Grunting, the man dropped to his knees.

–You something, he said. But I'm afraid you a bit too feisty for your own good.

He stood suddenly, pushed the woman backwards, and grabbed a beer bottle from the table. Holding it in the air above his bleeding head, he turned toward Carla.

–Don't leave this cabin or I'll kill you, the man said.

Carla closed her eyes and heard another shattering of glass and then a heavy thud that shook the cabin floor. Carla's heart raced through a long silence and then jumped at the next shattering of glass and the next. She tried to breathe; there was no breath inside her. Panicking, she opened her eyes.

He, bleeding heavily, crawled toward her. Beside him, the bloody woman crawled, too. Her hair had turned black. Blood ran down her neck. Side by side on their bellies the man and woman pulled themselves along toward her. Side by side, they moved under the table as they took the shortest route toward her. On elbows they pulled, with feet they pushed, edging closer, fallen, bloodied angels with urgent, opposing missions. Their hands reached out as the man, slightly ahead of the woman drew touching close.

–You leave this place, he said again. You dead.

Carla's breath exploded in a rush; her body shuddered violently.

She had never left that place. Never. That was clear to her now. It was as if she had swallowed that day, that man, that woman, that cabin, and they had stayed with her always.

How did I get home that day? Carla wondered. *Have I always been frozen by the fear and the blood crawling toward me? Why did my grandparents or the locals never know what happened? Weren't there two bodies on the floor to be discovered? Weren't other girls taken to the cabin? Surely one or two survived to tell their stories. And if I alone lived beyond my time there, haven't bodies been discovered or the missing searched for? Have I never left this place? Is it still going on and Carla, this Carla in the here and now, merely a wandering spirit about to walk in upon my younger self in a ghastly scene that has never ended and crawls toward me yet?*

She tethered Blaze to a tree near a clump of chicory. Reaching inside the saddlebag and inside the pocket of the flannel shirt, she grabbed the valium. She pressed the brown bottle tightly with her palm.

The cabin sat in the spreading silence as though waiting for her. The second of the three steps was missing as was some of the porch flooring. The door was open.

Being on the bottom step was easy, even moving to the top step quickened her pulse only slightly. Yet she was reluctant to let go of the post and push out onto the porch.

She was halfway across the porch when she felt something brush against her ankle.

Looking down, she saw the top of a small tree protruding slightly above the boards.

She had not before considered that something could be waiting for her under or over as well as within. She jerked her head upward, but except for cobwebs, wasp nests, and the

Generations

panpipe-like dwelling of dirt daubers the porch rafters were empty. She twirled around, but nothing was behind her, nothing she could see, and yet she was surrounded, afraid to move in any direction and terrified by the thought of not moving at all.

–Grab me and be done with it, she said and then eased through the doorway.

Inside, it was even darker. The fireplace, built of field stones, was lighter than the wood and looked milky white in the darkness. In the far corner to the left, an old, torn cloth hung down from the ceiling almost to the floor.

She followed the cloth down from the ceiling, wanting to maintain her distance, yet wanting to find a gap or tear large enough to reveal what was behind. Her eyes swept down the frayed material until they reached the floor and a pair of boots.

Carla backed against the wall hard enough to bang her head and shower her hair and shoulders with debris. Splinters pricked into her palms and fingers as she pressed into the wood, but she resisted the impulse to run.

–This, she told herself, is what I've been waiting for. There isn't enough room in this cabin for me and my fear. One or the other has to go.

One big bottle of medicine was in the cupboard, another in her hand.

–If I can pull back the cloth, I can do anything.

Curiously, she waited. She would not reach with pounding heart. She would give whatever was behind the cloth time to form itself, to gather itself into whatever hideousness or benevolence it possessed. Cautiously, she held back, knowing she must accept her breathing life as calmly as she would accept her breathless death. Ease came to her mind and a deep steadiness to her breathing. Slowly, she moved to her knees and bowing her head, she said softly, confidently the old childhood prayer, she had previously uttered in fear:

If She Should Die

And now I lay me down to sleep.
I pray Thee, God, my soul to keep.
If I should die before I wake.
I pray Thee, God, my soul to take.
If I should live for other days.
I pray Thee, God, to guide my ways.

She picked her place carefully, calculating where the kitchen table had been. On that chosen spot, she lay down, directly, as she figured, on the spot where the profusely bleeding woman and man had belly crawled toward her, he saying: You even think about leaving this place, I'll kill you.

She pressed down and then turned the bottle cap. With her fingers she pinched out a pill, the bitter bill she must or must not swallow. An old recipe: the bitter pharmacology taken to counter the bitterness of life. She rolled the pill between thumb and forefinger then brought it to her lips. Lightly, she rubbed the pill across her lips and then touched it with the tip of her tongue.

The old kitchen was washed clean with soft white moonlight. Beyond the curtain of the pie safe, she saw the boots. Perhaps the shelves were gone. Carla knew someone could be standing in the skeleton of the old pie safe, and she would see only the moonlit feet. She stared at the boots for the slightest sign of movement.

Carla's senses were too acute now to be fooled if there were empty spaces above the boots. There might be a ledge in the corner where someone could crouch. Perhaps the boots were a decoy. Perhaps the man and the woman gathered there still.

—Ridiculous, Carla said.

She spoke to convince herself she had nothing to fear, yet Carla knew that just when you think you're safe is the moment you're got.

—Do it or don't do it, she said.

Generations

She crushed the pill against the wood, pushed up from the floor, and started across the room. She felt eerily calm, her breathing steady.

She moved slowly; her mind was already made up. What she had feared most of her life was there, waiting. It had neither been conquered nor dismissed nor analyzed nor forgotten. Waiting behind the curtain, it was still terrifyingly and deadly real. The curtain, Carla knew, must go. That which had haunted and terrified her must be seen close and thoroughly.

As she touched the cloth, she was aware of how keen her senses were, how her living presence seemed to give the house a heart and a vibrancy. Even her fingernails seemed charged with sensation. Carla poked the center of the curtain inward but met no resistance. Then she gathered a ball of material into her fist and ripped downward.

—Damn, Blaze, she said as the mare drank from the mill pond, we made it.

From a distance the water wheel, which had been damaged by vandals, had looked workable. But as she looked more closely at the wheel, and at the large building itself, she knew that revival was unlikely, for time discards people and ways of life as though they had never been etched into a landscape or carved into a heart.

As Carla reined Blaze carefully away from the mill, she noticed the warmth of the air and found comfort in the swirls of fog gathering in low pockets of land.

Every time she stopped, she heard something. A limb breaking, a slosh of water, a rock kicked free and careening down the hill. Each time she would turn to examine the noise, but slowly, without panic.

110

If She Should Die

Things had turned around. What was behind her stayed way behind.

Dropping down into the hollow behind the barn, she paused. Her shadow and that of Blaze stretched down the hill, reaching toward the barns, the outbuildings, the house itself. The night felt expansive. The buildings all about her seemed to bulge with the breathing of what they contained, chickens, horses, goats. Though all things seemed to have a pulse, the house sat eerily still and, comparatively, breathless.

Leaving Blaze saddled in the stall, Carla walked toward the house. It sat quiet and stark white in the light of the full moon descending toward the western horizon. The small back porch sat in shadow.

Feeling the emptiness of the house, she opened the screen door and switched on the light.

Her grandfather's upper body lay slumped on the table. His right arm stretched across the table, his glasses clinched in his right hand near the overturned pepper shaker. His left arm dangled toward the floor. Carla stood quietly by the door, looking for, longing for breath from the slumped body. She breathed shallowly as though afraid to take any of the room's air.

Slowly he raised his head, opened his eyes, put on his glasses, fumbling even as he did so.

Carla moved toward him. His color was off, to use an expression he had always used. His face had a slight bluish cast. His breathing was ragged. She reached for the phone.

—Carla wait, he said. Here's where I want to be.

Carla dropped the phone.

She grabbed another chair and pulled it next to him, kissed him on his forehead, and took both of his hands in hers. She pressed her fingers between his, locking her hands with his. She took a deep breath, and another, steadying her breathing, seeming for the moment to steady his as well.

Generations

They sat there quietly, unmoving, in a moment of deep sharing forged from four steady hands on the kitchen table, granddaughter and grandfather in close huddle as the night gave slowly to the first light above the ridgeline.

Fireflies

I was six years old when it happened that August day seventy years ago. My sister Eve was staying with Addie, and having our parents all to myself I ran in celebration on the front porch. Around my mouth was the dried brown stain of apple butter. Ma was sewing an enormous red shirt that would have swaddled me completely. It dangled from the rocker. Pa stood with one foot on the porch rail, his deep blue eyes set on some distant point.

I ran up beside him, threw my foot on the bottom rail, and pretended to set my eyes on the distance. He saw me and smiled, then turned to watch Jake rise into view at a gallop.

I saw nothing unusual in that. Jake was our tenant farmer. Ma saw nothing unusual either. She walked over to Pa and held the red shirt out to him. He frowned as he bent and put it on.

Jake slowed to a lope through the orchard and beside the barn, then came up fast to the porch. He pulled an envelope out of his hat.

—What does it say? Pa asked.

Jake blushed. He couldn't read and that was Pa's way of kidding him. Jake didn't like to be teased. Ma'd told Pa about that before.

—Give it here, Jake, Pa said and reached for the paper. His sleeve hung down to his knuckles.

Generations

    –Let me have the shirt, Mister Roberts, Ma said. I didn't get it quite right.

    He laughed and took it off.

    –Makes me feel sissy-like standing before God and the world in an unmade shirt.

    –I got no pattern for it, she said, and you wouldn't let me fit you. It was the best I could do.

    –It's going to be pretty, Zell. Going to be just fine.

    Already though he was into something. His voice dropped off the way a rooster's crow does when you fling a stick at him.

    –What's that writing about, Mister Roberts? Ma asked.

    He didn't say anything. Didn't ever say anything to her again.

    –Jake, go saddle Galler.

    Ma could have asked Pa until the sun fell, but he wasn't going to tell her anything he didn't want to. She sat down and started ripping out the sleeve but couldn't pay much mind to her work. Except for tugging at his mustache he didn't fidget much. Stood there straight as you please studying God knows what.

    Ma pulled a few stitches, then put them right back in, leaving the shirt just like it was when he dropped it off his back. I reached inside. It was still warm. Pa carried a lot of heat about him.

    –I'm going, too, I said.

    When Jake came out of the barn, Pa put the new shirt on. Jake led Galler up beside the porch, and Pa slid into the saddle and took off at a trot. Jake followed on Black while I kicked and screamed at being left.

    Ma reached for me, and her sewing basket went tumbling. She pulled me to the barn. She was panting as she fitted the bridle on the mare. That's all she used. She left the saddle on the table by the stall. The mare jerked at the bit, then calmed a little when Ma straightened the headstall. Ma hopped on behind me.

Galloping, we caught Pa and Jake a ways past Jake's house. Pa didn't look at us.

–Jake, I don't think they should go, he said.

Jake didn't know what to say. He looked at us, then at Pa.

–You want me to do something about it, Mister Roberts.

–They don't need to go.

–Did you hear that, Miss Roberts?

–Yes, she said, continuing to ride alongside.

–She heard it, Mister Roberts.

–She ain't turned around, Jake.

–Maybe we could ride faster, Jake suggested.

They heeled into the sides of their horses and moved ahead. Ma couldn't catch them, but she laid back and followed.

We rode up into some country I'd never seen before. The river kept drawing tighter and tighter. Must've been getting to where the Chattahoochee springs from, when we came into this wide grove of apples.

I watched Pa bobbing up and down as he rode through the shadows. At a mill at the far end, folk started climbing into wagons and buggies. Some started toward us on horseback, but all were too far away to be heard.

It was peaceful where we were. There wasn't any noise but the squeak of the men's saddles, and hoofs pounding the ground. We could see the folk at the far end spreading out and riding fast for us.

I felt good bouncing along the bare back of the mare as I watched the horse work her head. We closed on Jake and Pa. I leaned back against Ma and watched how straight Pa sat as he rode.

Jake was wanting to go back. He turned, raised his eyes at me, scratched his neck, and leaned way back in the saddle like

Generations

that would hold him back. It didn't. Black went on as steady as you please, till we come up to a road.

Coming down off the mountain was a Palomino, prancing tail, almost dancing, pulling a shiny, black buggy. The man who was driving the buggy had one leg out to the side. His boot shone bright in the sunlight as he drew near us. Beside him on the seat was a valise made of velvet with daises stitched on the side. It was a pretty thing. Him, too. He had a goatee. A monocle hung out of his coat pocket. He leaned forward and let the reins fall sassily.

–I told your Pa they's gonna be trouble over that woman, Ma whispered to me.

I saw that Pa was watching the fancy man, too, watching him hard and then staring at that valise like it was brimming with snakes. I didn't see any woman.

–Well, the fancy man said, you come.

–You knew I'd come, Pa said.

–How formal you want to hold it? the fancy man said, and he raised that monocle to his eyes and drew his brow down to hold it.

–What are you two up to? Ma asked.

A big circle of people had gathered round.

–You get them out of the way, the fancy man said, motioning to Ma and me; his monocle fell to his coat.

–They'll git, Pa said.

We did. She backed the mare just like she was a scolded little girl.

Pa called Jake, and the fancy man called in a toothless wrinkled man who wore a crushed hat. The fancy one kept his seat while the other three dismounted and stood beside him. He opened the valise, and they all looked inside. Pa reached in and pulled out a pistol. I don't know what kind it was. It had a short barrel and a handle that looked so slim it was bound to be loose in

Fireflies

a hand as big as Pa's. He handed it to Jake, who examined it and nodded his head.

The circle broke and formed two rows. Jugs of early cider lined the sides of some of the wagons. The mules and horses nibbled orchard grass while everyone watched as Pa's foe jumped down and took a pistol from the valise.

Jake paced a distance off from the wagon and then dug the heel of his boot hard into that clay soil. He rocked his heel slowly back and forth. The toe of the boot swung evenly to and fro.

I didn't count the paces of either man. When I looked some distance beyond Jake, there was another toe rocking as the toothless, crushed-hat man worked the clay hard with his booted heel. Both men rocked their boot toes soft and easy, but I could tell they pressed hard with the heels. Both those men moved their lips to grins and looked at each other. The grins and the looks were hard. They still had those hard grins when they finished. They gathered the flesh up around their mouths and spit into the holes they had made. Then they backed away from their work, folded their arms over their chests and stood there.

The fancy man stepped to the toothless man's spit. Pa dug his heels into Jake's spit. The crowd stood still as firewood awaiting the fall of the ax.

I can't hold my hand as still now as Jake and the toothless man and the hundred other people stood. I couldn't hold it as still then. Except for the horses shivering to the flies, everything, but me, was solid, mute. I trembled like it was the first day of winter. Ma squeezed her arms tight around me and leaned her bosom across the top of my head. She whispered something, but I couldn't still myself to her words.

Pa and the fancy man faced each other. Both worked their left hands hard, opening and closing, opening and clenching like they were trying to get the right grip on cow tits before pumping milk. Their faces were set one on the other. Both raised their

Generations

eyebrows like they were working to get all out of their eyesight they could.

I couldn't stand looking. For a second I turned away. People were standing about the hillside, too. They didn't move; they stood rooted to the hill like trees. A light breeze stirred the leaves, then it died down.

I turned back to the two men. The air about them was still as all the people watching.

Sweat stood out on Pa right above his mustache. The fancy one grinned and fiddled with his pistol. Then he heisted his head like he had a twitch and slid his right foot forward like a dancer. In that moment, there was no human sound. I heard water running in the stream. Heard mules and horses chomping and their tails swatting at flies. Saw red in Pa's mustache that shone in sungleam, and his eyes hard as pebbles as he watched that fancy man.

I watched the golden glitter of the fancy man's monocle chain. I saw that monocle bright as a diamond shining across that fancy man's right eye and then as quick as I saw it whole it was shivered to motes. They twinkled in the air like lost stars, and something as black as the fancy man's shoes splashed out and mingled. I rocked from the explosion from Pa's pistol. Smoke billowed soft in the air.

Around the fallen fancy man, grass turned dark. The pistol's report faded slow.

Ma looked at Jake and reeled around hard. Jake shoved Pa up on Galler, flew up on Black, and we pounded through the orchard. I looked back, but no one was coming after us. They had all closed round the fancy man.

We rode fast and no one talked. The white river widened and the yellow in the sky narrowed.

When we slowed to let Pa and Jake catch us, I saw that Pa looked pale.

Fireflies

We swung over to the river and dropped the reins and let the horses drink. Their hoofs looked bright like stones in the rushing water. Pa hung his head like the horses. His breath was hard as theirs.

–Gonna be a hard winter, Ma said.

She got down and lifted me to a rock at the edge. The sun was low and the air chilly. Water swirled around the hems of her dress. Water oozed out of the fabric.

It was still foaming as she lifted it. Jake stared at her white petticoat.

–Tired of seeing your dirty mouth, she said to me.

–Why'd Pa do that?

–One, two, three, just like that, Jake said. He grinned like we all needed some humor. And yours, he said to Pa, was the two dug deep.

–I only heard two shots, Ma said.

There might have been three or two or a million. I didn't know. The first one deafened me to the others.

–I heard only one, I said.

–Close your mouth, Ma said as she scrubbed my mouth. It felt like the dried apple butter and part of my skin were erased by her abrasions. My face burned a long time afterwards.

It was almost dark when we got home. A firefly lit up by the hornbeam above the fence line. As we turned and headed for the house, a swarm of fireflies fanned out and flickered gold above the hay field. I leaned over to grab one, but Ma hiked me up.

–Ain't got no time for that, she said.

At the house, Ma lifted me off and onto the porch. She ran in and lit a lantern and brought it back outside.

Pa'd already made up his mind what had to be done. He went to the barn and got Jake to hitch Galler and Black to the wagon.

–Them's tired horses, Jake. You be easy with them.

Generations

—Yeah, he said.
—Know what I'm figuring on? Pa asked him.
—No, he said.

Pa took Jake by the arm and led him back to the stall where the two trunks that were with Pa when he first came to the county were stored. They were painted black and had brass locks and bindings.

Pa pulled one out a little.
—Now what we gonna do? Jake asked.
Pa got inside the trunk and curled up.
—Put it on the wagon.
Jake looked at him, and Pa knew he wasn't thinking right.
—I was trying it for size, Pa said, not to be caught figuring wrong.

He got out of the trunk and gave Jake a twenty-dollar gold piece. Jake grinned when he got it. Ma and I fretted about that. This is what Pa told him:

—Jake, drive me to the depot. Wait till the train's loading before closing the trunk. Give the gold to the conductor to get me on the train and watch me to Atlanta. You see that the trunk's opened as soon as it gets in the baggage car. I'll get off in Atlanta.

Jake and Pa put the trunk on the wagon. Then Pa climbed back in.

Ma threw me up on the wagon and told me to look inside. In all the years since, in all the closings of coffin lids, I have never seen anything as frightful as that. Him alive and hunched up in a red shirt. His eyes moving back and forth almost as if they were out of control, speeding almost, except for that one moment, that one long moment when they held me with such heat I began to sweat. I turned away as Ma closed the lid, leaving the latch open so he could breath. Closing him up live and worried stirred my heart, and something in me said I would never again see the

Fireflies

strong man who stood high with a foot braced against the porch rail, never again see how he bounced easy and light in the saddle.

We jumped down, and the black trunk waited lonesome in the wagon.

Ma lit a small lantern and put it in the frame at the rear of the wagon.

–It might be better without the light, Jake said.

–You keep it lit till past your place. I can't stand to see him off without something shining, Ma said.

Jake nodded and took the horses slow out of the barn. Ma and I ran along behind until Jake got to the road. We watched the light diminish until it was no bigger than the glow of a firefly.

Jake had been gone three hours when a gang of men came riding up to the porch. They ran in the house, then searched in the barn.

–Where's your two men, one asked.

Everywhere I looked I saw Pa hunched down in the trunk, that red shirt puckered at his shoulder.

The man asked again, but Ma paid him no mind.

–Crazy woman, the man said, and they took off, galloped south.

The next night, way past midnight, Jake returned.

Seeing him didn't stop my mind from churning about the things he might've done.

–Let me have that gold piece back, Ma said.

Jake reached for his pocket, then stopped.

–I ain't got that, he grinned. Give it to the conductor man.

–Did Mister Roberts get off the train in Atlanta?

–I don't know, Jake said and grinned. The conductor wouldn't let me stay with the trunk.

Ma looked at me.

Generations

—I gotta get this little un to bed, she said.

—Where's Pa? I screamed. Where's Eve?

—You know she's spending a week with Addie. Don't you fret none about your sister or Mister Roberts either.

She took off my clothes and helped me into my nightgown.

That was a summer of fireflies. They came in multitudes and hovered thick night after night. Even in early October they hadn't diminished. They stayed until the first hard frost, the night before school started. That night I dreamed of Pa in the trunk. But there wasn't no complete man, hardly a partial one. Just two hard eyes lit up like fireflies down in the bottom of the trunk, the way fireflies like to hover on the floor of a cove.

I woke up sweating.

—Ma, I screamed. I can't find him.

She hurried into the room. I could feel her sit beside me on the bed.

—Light a lantern, I pleaded.

—No, she said. You've got to sleep.

I told her about my drowsy thoughts.

—Well, she said, Mister Roberts should be back soon.

I could tell that she was looking away from me.

—You've been saying that for two months. What if he isn't back soon? I asked.

—If he's not, she whispered, You can spend evenings chasing fireflies until you catch your Pa.

I lay in bed in the cold, dark room. Outside it was cold and dark, too. I was scared and tired, my face still tender from sweat as my body slowly yielded to exhaustion. I watched in my mind as the wagon with the black trunk rolled away from the barn, watched until the lantern grew smaller and smaller, until it was no bigger than a firefly, watched it go back and forth from firefly to lantern, until the firefly lantern exploded into a thousand fireflies lighting up above the ground mist. I searched for the one that was the lantern. It was there. There. No. There it was. No, I'd lost it again. Lost in the legion of fireflies.

Pears

The old man visited once a year, always in August, but this time was different. He would, he said, take the boy back with him. The boy's parents didn't believe it, nor did the boy; yet a tightness clamped them as though they sensed what they refused to affirm: no matter how hard they worked to make the visit normal, something—an old man's obstinacy or merely time itself—tore at the design. Upheaval raced through the mother's mind as she and her son pulled weeds from the base of the pear tree, leaving a circle of brown sand.

—That's what all of Texas looks like, she said. You wouldn't want to spend the rest of the summer there.

The boy couldn't understand why his parents made such a fuss. He was certain the meticulous care they gave to the cleaning of the house and yard was their way of venting frustration about the impending guest. They had even argued about the pears before deciding to, as his father said: Let him have the goddamn things.

On the morning of the old man's arrival, the boy was sent out bearing a white bowl trimmed with gold. As he walked, grass clippings sprang like grasshoppers to his bare legs.

Generations

The yard they had cleaned the previous afternoon looked like a battlefield, the neatly trimmed lawn now scarred with depressions that marked the fall of pears. Some had hit with such force that they exploded, forcing the grass down into the soft soil. A lively squadron of yellow jackets tumbled over the bashed earth, blitzed the defective pears, and lay siege to the grass clippings, pine needles, and bruised, rotting pears dumped beside the street. So telling was the transformation that the boy veered away from the pear tree, squatted on his haunches, and stared at the trash pile and at the yellow jackets crawling in and out of the crevices in the battered pears.

–Not that. No, Crawler. The good pears, his mother shouted from the porch. Can't you do anything right?

Startled, he put the bowl over his chest and watched her as she stood on the porch. In one hand she held a frying pan and in the other a dish towel, which revolved quickly and roughly inside the pan.

–Fast now, you hear. Go along. I need you to come in and give me a hand with the dishes.

The screen door banged shut, and she was gone. Sometimes he liked her best that way. He wondered if it was a sin.

Closing his eyes, he walked away from the trash pile. He grimaced when his bare foot came down on the side of a pear, but he knew, also, the more intense pain of the stabbing stem. Squeezing his eyelids tight, he didn't stop walking until his feet touched sand. Extending his right foot, he touched the trunk, then moved the foot back. Digging his toes into the soft, moist sand, he slowly arched his back and lifted his head. He opened his eyes and smiled at the web of thick, green leaves. Shafts of sunlight pierced through the openings—bright, insubstantial bracing for the bent and laden limbs.

He went around the tree until he found the limb he wanted. He grasped it with one hand and protected his head with the other. He pulled the limb and pushed it up, the way kids pump their hands in hopes a trucker will sound his horn. Dew splashed about his face, leaves rustled, and the pears swayed in a wild ride, jumping, twisting, yet held by the limb. Disappointed, he let go and stared as the limb once more sprang upwards. He watched a pear above the limb, a pear that didn't move. All the others jostled and nodded.

The boy was fascinated by the way a pear breaks from the tree, the way you don't even know it's free until you realize it's no longer jiggling like the others that dance above then below the limb. The loosened pear hangs in a brief state of suspension before it falls to earth, or as happened this time, into a boy's waiting hands.

Watching him, his mother longed for a camera that would really freeze time. Would hold a son like hers forever at eleven, before adolescence and its fumbling needs altered him forever. Once you see what it's like, she had told him, you'll wish you had taken your time about such sorry business as growing up. And you might also wish your grandfather would stay in Texas, if that's what he wants to call home.

–Crawler, quit shaking that tree! she yelled.

He didn't look, but he could tell the voice came from the kitchen window. He hid the caught pear near the trunk and went about the gathering. When he had ten large pears stacked in a pyramid on the grass, he walked back toward the street and the hovering, crawling yellow jackets. Reaching into the trash pile where they were thickest, he took out the pear that had been their favorite. They had nibbled it until it looked like a hungry man had taken two good bites.

He put that pear in the bottom of the bowl, piled the pyramid on top and walked into the house. The screen door slammed shut.

Generations

–What you think I've been doing all morning? Get out there and brush off your feet.

The door reopened slightly, and two bare feet scraped back and forth across the doorjamb.

At three o'clock in the afternoon, they gathered in the living room to await the grandfather's arrival. The boy waited with his face pressed against the front screen door, pressed tight enough that the wire made small, square imprints on his forehead, and a bit of loose, black paint stuck to the middle. The boy's mother leaned against an oversized chair positioned between the window and the thick, blue, floor-length drapes. Her pale fingers pinched the molding of the window, though she was unaware they were doing anything more than resting. Through the window she saw, as the boy did through the door, the straw-filled S-shaped walk.

Across the street was a house of identical shape but different color. As a diversion, they watched Sarah Boland beat her brother with a peach switch as he screamed for his mother's help. Unheeded, he appealed to a higher authority.

–Oh, Mother, God, Oh Mother, God, stop her!

Mrs. Boland, a white apron curved across her fat belly, banged an empty pie tin against the metal railing of the porch. A kitten scampered off to the hedge, with a dog in quick pursuit.

–You get in here this minute, Sarah, she shouted. Don't you ever let me catch you doing nothing like that again.

As she approached her mother, the girl put her elbows against her head as though expecting to be hit, then squeezed past her mother into the darkness of the house. The mother turned to follow her, leaving Johnny Boland to cry alone. Lying on his side, he wrenched a handful of grass from the lawn and wiped it across his eyes and cheeks.

—Maybe I shouldn't say it, Crawler's mother said, but there's not much to those folks. Then as quickly as she said it, she was again quietly staring through the window. The father sat asleep with his head tilted back on the sofa, each breath giving a slight, momentary curl to his upper lip.

The sleeping father, the waiting mother, and the boy, almost as motionless as a fresco. Around them hung the strong sweet odor of overripe pear. The boy knew that the aromatic pear he had chosen for the bottom of the bowl was nearer to rotten than he had intended. He resolved to choose one less brown and bruised next time. He wondered if his mother would say anything about what sat in the bottom of her golden bowl.

The boy was transfixed by staring through the little black boxes of the screen, by the fragmented world revealed. Above the shimmering black roof of the house across the street, heat waves wavered and disappeared in a hazy blue sky.

The boy emerged from his trance and saw, parked a little too high on the carefully cut lawn, a black car sitting motionless in front of him. The dust of the street rose skyward like the heat waves. Nothing could be heard but the car itself: the squeaky door, which the old man shoved open, and the water gurgling through the radiator and hissing and foaming at the cap.

—Franklin, Franklin, the woman called.

The man stirred, then stretched.

—Daddy's here.

—'Bout time, he said, rubbing a finger across his upper lip.

—He looks really feeble now, she sighed.

—What did you expect? He's old. He was old when you were born. He can't be bellowing about forever.

The boy knew what was coming next when his father turned toward him.

—You and your mother are both lucky to be alive, he said. Not many become fathers at the age he did.

Generations

The boy watched the slow movement of his grandfather, but it didn't seem any slower than it had the year before. Even then his grandfather had held on to the car as he made his way to the walk.

The black cane with the gold knob stuck out the window on the passenger side. As the old man reached for it, the boy was shoved into the oversized chair. He looked up into his mother's angry eyes.

—Crawler, didn't you hear your father ask you to move? she asked, measuring the words for effect.

—No, Ma'am.

—You better start looking and you better start listening. You better straighten up in general if you know what's good for you.

The boy's mother turned to follow his father outside. The boy leaned his head across the arm of the chair and looked at the window. Near the bottom he saw where he had missed a smear. He rubbed it with the drape. Through the polished, clear pane, he watched his father take the cane and put his forearm under the old man's armpit. In the rear, like a rudder, his mother steered them toward the door. No one said a word or offered a hug. Something was empty there, the boy knew. So big and empty you could throw a bowl of pears right through it.

Though the curved walkway wasn't very long, it seemed to the boy that several minutes passed before his grandfather started up the steps. As the old man, assisted by the boy's parents, reached the top step, the boy opened the screen door and faced him.

The old man scraped a scruffy wingtip across the concrete step. He pushed his son-in-law's forearm down and away, then leaned forward, freeing himself from the guiding hand of his daughter. With extreme concentration, he stepped onto the porch and stood before his grandson. The old man grinned.

Pears

The boy glanced at his parents. They were bending forward as if they expected the old man to topple any moment. Then the boy looked at the hairless arms moving toward him, the arms lined with gnarled veins and dotted with brown spots. The boy felt his own heart beating hard as he looked at the man reaching for him, felt the muscle beat so heavily in the cavern of his chest that his flat belly quivered.

–You better hurry on into the house before you pitch backwards on your head, the mother warned, but before she had finished, the boy and his grandfather embraced. The boy was almost as tall as his grandfather, a man so scrawny that the boy felt he would crack if squeezed too hard.

–I swear you're a foot taller, the old man said proudly. You keep going and you'll have that sharp-tongued mother of yours looking up to you.

–He's got a long way to go for that, the woman said. She laughed as an afterthought.

The old man smelled of Dentyne. The boy walked him to the armchair upholstered in a pattern of red roses. The old man reached for the cane and placed it diagonally from the corner of the chair to the ottoman. He sat down beside the cane and settled back into the chair. The boy lifted his grandfather's legs and placed them across the cane. While the boy unlaced the old shoes, his grandfather pulled out a dirty handkerchief and swept it across his ancient face.

His teeth looked like chipped yellow pebbles stuck in mud. His face was dotted with small red spots.

The boy looked around at the waxed hardwood floor, the magazines stacked neatly in the rack. Sunlight came cleanly through the windows and cast images of misshapen panes on the green braided rug in front of the fireplace. The boy looked in the shaft of light for the dance of dust, but there was no motion. The air, clean, ripe with pear scent. It made him feel good.

Generations

    –You do look chipper, the boy's father said. Must be some old Texas girl got you looking so perky.
    –Yeah, you're looking good, the woman said as she stared at the gold knob of his cane and handed him a pear.
    He took the chewing gum out of his mouth and rolled it into a tight ball, which he balanced on the arm of the chair. His daughter frowned.
    As the old man ate the pear, the red spots on his face receded.
    –Ain't no trouble, am I?
    –No. You don't cause extra work, if that's what you mean, his daughter answered.
    The boy's mouth fell open.
    –Crawler, can't you look halfway intelligent?
    –Yes, Mother, he said and closed his mouth.
    –He's getting to be a big whippersnapper, his grandfather said.
    –Yeah, the mother answered forlornly. Before you know it, he'll be gone.
    –Maybe now's the time.
    –You listen! she screamed. If you came this far to talk about that, you might as well get back in the car and drive your old self back to...
    –Hold on, hold on, her husband said. Nobody's talking about nothing.
    The old man, again splotched with red, tilted two fingers toward his mouth. The boy got up and walked into the kitchen. He waited to hear if something would be said. There was nothing. He got two ice cubes and ran a glass of water, listening again after turning off the tap. He waited to hear a comprehensible conversation from the dead living room. He took a deep breath and walked toward the silence. Cold beads trickled down the glass, and ice floated just beneath the surface.

Pears

Reaching out for the glass, his grandfather winked at him.

—Crawler, his mother said. You go out and play awhile. We've got some important talking to do.

—I don't see why the boy can't stay, too. After all, it's about him.

—Listen, Pops, I'm saying the way it is. Now you get, Crawler.

The boy looked to his father for a different opinion but saw he was staring out the window.

—We're waiting as usual, his mother said.

The boy left the room and went into the kitchen. He opened the drawer of ice picks, plunder from the summer his father, as a teenager, had worked at the ice and coal company during its last year of existence. When the boy was ten and the long-deserted plant was being torn down, his father took him to see the large vats where water from the underground river and distilled water were blended to create a clear, delicious ice. They stood on the old scales, father and son, then wandered through the roofless cubicle that was once the office.

—The day after the plant closed, the boy's father had said, pointing at the wall, Mr. Tal walked into this office before daylight, propped his chair against that wall, as though he was going to take a nap, then stuck both barrels of a sawed-off shotgun in his mouth, like the gun was a popsicle. Plunging his hand down into the clutter of black, wooden handles, the boy remembered the deep, irregular, blacker-than-dirt stain on the office wall, a stain left by a man's last, surrendering act.

The boy wondered if that's how life really is. One morning you wake up to a life not worth living, and the next morning and for all the remaining history of time, you don't wake at all. And while you lie in the earth, the wall and the blood you left on it collapse as well.

The boy lifted an ice pick out of the drawer. Standing in front of the sink, he balanced the point on the tip of his finger.

Generations

He could feel pressure as he pushed down on the handle, first easy, then harder, until the skin was punctured and a bead of bright blood popped to the surface. He put the ice pick down and squeezed his finger until a small pool of blood covered the tip. As it spilled over the side, he turned on the tap. His finger throbbed, but the bleeding slowed under the running water.

Before his mother could get in the kitchen to see what he had done, he grabbed the ice pick and rushed out to the pear tree. From there, he saw Johnny Boland sitting on the steps across the street. The boy called for Johnny to come to the tree.

–Bring Sarah, too, he shouted.

Johnny finished his popsicle before shouting back: We can't play with anybody the rest of the day. Mommy says she'll kill us if we cause her any more trouble.

–Hush up your lies, Johnny, the mother yelled. I ain't said no such thing.

Propped against the pear tree, the boy waited. He thought about walking down the hill to the small creek where he caught crayfish, built mud dams, and launched flotillas of sticks. Maybe he'd keep going until he reached the livestock barn. He'd gone there once. What had struck him most was the way the eyes of the auctioneer jumped around and the speed of his mouth. The driven steer was frantic in the ring while the buyers gave secret motions. One tugged an ear, another raised eyeglasses. Each motion too brief to be seen by the other bidders, yet scooped up instantly by the roving eye of the auctioneer. I've got thirty, thirty, now five, thirty-five, give me four say four, got forty, need... Sometimes the chant continued after the animal was prodded through the exit gate, the auctioneer staring at the bidders, and the bidders looking at the empty ring littered with sawdust.

Leaning against the pear tree, the boy looked up and saw his father at the kitchen window. His father nodded his head as if to

Pears

say he, too, wondered how long the two would haggle over the situation. The boy didn't mind not being involved in the deliberations; he had no answer. He wanted only to be left alone. Let time take care of things. Isn't that what time is for?

He played listlessly through one game of mumblety-peg, getting all the way to Spank the Baby, but had no desire to carry the game any further. With the ice pick in his back pocket, he was walking toward the creek when his grandfather called to him from the back bedroom, called him back into the house.

–What did you decide? the boy asked.

–It's not for me to decide for you. We're just talking about the last two weeks of summer. You sound like we're plotting the rest of your life.

–This is the rest of my life.

–What is?

–Whatever's left of it.

–My God. Sometimes you talk like you're old enough to be my grandfather. Fact is, you're not even fully sprouted.

–Reckon I'm still growing?

–Sure you are. Do the right things, you'll get big and strong. Eat the globular strength of pears, I always say. It worked for me.

–It did? the boy asked, looking at the tiny man.

–You should have seen me when I was young. He flexed his arm. Are you going to play football this year?

–Mother says I might get hurt.

–Mother said, Mother says, Mother said. It's people like that drove me to Texas. He leaned toward the boy and held out his hands. Come to Texas with me.

–I'll have to think about it.

–Think? That's what she wants you to do. That's what you've done most of your life. Give up thinking for a while. Act.

Generations

Remember when you were in kindergarten how scared you were of those marble gargoyles near the top of the bank? Remember how I took you up on the roof and we looked down on them? What did we see?

–Their heads piled high with pigeon poop.

–'Poor things,' you said as you looked down. See what I'm getting at. Taking those steps to the roof led you to pity what you once feared.

–You know when I was a boy, the old man said as he rubbed a green pear back and forth between his palms, my parents didn't send me out with bowls to collect pears. When we had too many kittens running in the barn, they sent me out to kill them. The only way I could do it—and my parents went along with me on this—was to give them a chance. I'd put each one in a sack, twist it shut, and tie it off with tobacco twine. Then I'd set them out in a line behind the barn. Those that thought about what they needed to do, thought and thought until the air ran out. I buried them, still in the sacks. Those that used their claws, their teeth, their fury shredded their coffins and ran, angry as hell, back into the barn. Later they lapped milk and purred while I shoveled dirt on the thinkers.

The old man reached into his pocket and pulled out a rotten strand of string.

–Your momma's gonna so muddle you that you'll think nothing but her thoughts. Break free. Don't let her diminish you. Claw yourself out a name that gives you respect, not one she uses to ridicule you. Don't let her call you Crawler. Don't let me.

–I've always been called that. I don't like it, though.

–Then get another name, like that Langhorne bull who tossed aside Samuel Clemens and made his own Mark. It's your life, put your brand on it. Call yourself Strider or Walker or Stomper. Ain't that better?

—Make her say it. Tell her you're changing, and you'd like her to be a helpful part of it. Then if she won't listen to desire and reason, take action. Spit on her. Spit on anybody who calls you Crawler. Me included.

A smile broke across the boy's face. Then he giggled.

—Funny, isn't it? Funny to imagine yourself having the upper hand for once. Tell you what. You better grab and claw and keep that hand up there reaching, he said, handing the boy the frayed twine. This came off the last kitten bag I ever tied.

The old hand went back to the pocket. The old man wished he had more to give the boy, but his wealth was example and artifact. He pulled out a coin.

—What's this? he asked.

—Easy, the boy said as he tilted the gold coin in the sunlight. It's a coin. The metal smooth on both sides, not the slightest indication of scratch or impression. The boy couldn't tell what was up and down, what was head, what tails.

—Been handled and pressed so much, his grandfather said, that it's worn plumb smooth.

—Where'd you get it?

—It was my great-grand, he paused. Doesn't matter if mother or father. Your great-great-great, but that doesn't matter either. The important thing here is the coin has been clutched enough to erase the engraving. You can't tell its worth. It's spent so much of life between someone's thumb and forefinger that there's no tail to sit on nor face to spit with. You know what I'm saying by giving you the twine and the coin?

—I do, the boy said.

—You're smart. Remember a body needs a head and a tail to wiggle through this crooked world. And what you lose of the body, what you need beyond, you have to make up in spirit.

—Is it really gold? the boy asked, looking in his palm.

Generations

—If you think so. Ain't much true in this world if you don't believe it so.

He leaned across and kissed his grandson.

Staring at the indecipherable coin, the boy didn't see the stark red of the sunset.

—Flyer, the boy said proudly, remembering the way the pear had been jerked about, then steadied itself before springing off into the air and down to his waiting hands.

—Let's try this, then, the old man said. You go get some water and tell my witch of a daughter that your name is Flyer.

—I'll ask her to call me that.

—Nothing wrong with asking and explaining, but lay out the consequences for her if she doesn't go along with the new ways.

—I don't know that I could do that.

—You gotta do something different. You hear me, the old man said in a louder voice. Do something different, or you'll be sitting in this room old as me and having a 100 and umpteen plus year old woman in the next room telling you what to do. And if you keep doing everything she says, there will come the day she won't even have to be alive to run your life. You'll be jumping to the commands of a dead woman.

The boy walked slowly down the hall. In his right front pocket a piece of twine and a smooth gold coin; in his back pocket, a black-handled ice pick.

The boy's mother stood beside the stove, snapping ears of corn in two and dropping them into a pot of boiling water. The boy lifted the lid of another pot. The dark foam of peas retreated, revealing a hard brown crust on the upper rim. The odor of cornbread drifted up from the oven, and deep red barbecue sauce bubbled around pork chops.

—What have you two been talking about?

The boy got two glasses from the cabinet. As he held them under the tap, he tried to think of something to say to her, of a way to announce his proud, new name.

–When water runs down the sides, the glass is full. Don't you know that, Crawler?

His fingers tightened around the glass.

–Has he finished talking that foolishness about going to Texas?

–He doesn't make it sound foolish.

–It is, Crawler. Don't listen to him. He talks nonsense most of the time, and if you've got any sense you know it. Going off cross-country with that old man. It's not safe. You see how slow he is. He'd plow through three red lights before his dull brain could get his foot to the brake. I wouldn't let you go around the block with him. And I say that even if he is my father. And soon as your father gets in from work you'll see that your parents are in total agreement on this.

–We haven't decided about the trip yet.

His mother's face turned red as the sauce.

–Is it for you to decide? she said.

He didn't look at her as he started for the bedroom.

–You haven't answered my question.

He could sense that she was moving toward him, moving with that dark red face and an ear of waving corn. He walked faster, but he didn't look back.

–No, he said. It's not for me to decide. Behind him, the steps diminished.

–Heard some crawling but didn't hear any asking or spitting or flying, the old man said as the boy walked into the room. He motioned for the boy to put the glasses on the dresser.

–I thought you were thirsty, the boy said, startled by his grandfather's appearance.

Generations

The old man had taken off his shirt. From his arms, remnants of muscle, like mummified fruit, hung wrinkled and brown. Sitting in the rocking chair by the opened window, he spread a towel across his bare upper torso. Another towel lay across his lap, the ends of the towel draping to the floor.

It was early evening. In the growing darkness outside the window, the pear leaves were barely visible.
—You remind me of that tree. The way the white blooms come, then the new leaves, half green, half red, like they don't know whether to stop or rush out into life.
The boy held half a glass of water in his hands. The other half was in his mouth, pushing his cheeks out like he had mumps. The old man looked at the full cheeks and smiled.
—What are you waiting for?
The boy shook his head.
—You don't want to spit on me anymore, is that it? I can take it, Crawler. And I believe you're man enough to try. Crawler, Crawler, Crawler, Crawler, Crawler. Come on, I'm getting tired and hungry. Crawler, Crawler, Crawler—
The boy took a deep breath and forced the water to the front of his mouth. The water broke through his lips and splattered against the side of the old man's face.
—That's ten in a row, the old man laughed. I believe you've got the hang of it, Flyer.
The boy laughed, too. He selected the driest handkerchief and started wiping the wet face.
—Teaching sure is messy business, the old man said.
—But you wanted me to do it.
The old man stood up and balanced against the wall. You've got to know you can do it, Flyer. Whatever it takes to free yourself, you gotta know you can do.
He walked to the boy and kissed him on the forehead.

–Going with me?
–I'm not sure. I think so.
–I'm talking about supper.
–Oh, the boy blushed.

The old man tossed the wet towels on the floor.

–Now, he said, this is the real test. You've got to walk down the hallway and find that woman who's been cutting away at you for years. This won't stop her shears forever, but it may slow them down.

She stood in the kitchen.

–My name is Flyer, he said. I'd like you and Daddy to call me Flyer.

–What?

–I don't want to be called Crawler anymore. I'm eleven years old. I don't need a name with training wheels on it.

–You shut up that foolishness, she said, then paused.

In that moment, a strange elation shook his body. He had said what he had wanted to say, and more important he had said what he had felt. Not lines fed him by his grandfather, not words to assuage his mother's anger—he had expressed what he felt. And that simple act, it seemed to the boy, added pounds to his frame.

–You shut your mouth, Crawler, his mother warned.

–Flyer, he said.

–Crawler! she shouted.

Shouts last a long time. That's one thing the boy had learned. If you don't flinch, if you don't run, you can steady yourself. He had options. He could return quietly to his grandfather's classroom; he could stand before his mother forever, mute, frozen.

Generations

He moved his hand slowly and brushed against his pocket, feeling the impressions of coin and twine. He moved that same hand behind his back and clasped the handle of the ice pick, his hand throbbing open and shut, open and shut. His neck muscles tightened; his heart went wild. He pursed his lips and blew outward. A dribble of spit ran down his chin as a few drops splattered against the wall and a few landed on her apron.

Hurrying through the kitchen, the boy sensed her pursuit. Soon, he knew, she would pounce; yet he felt stronger, as though his chest had swelled to the dimension of shirt, his hips to the contour of jeans. In that expansion, he could feel against his hip the metal of the ice pick, the wood of its handle.

His mother said nothing more, but followed him across the kitchen. Her eyes wide, a wry smile plastered to her red face. He stood by the back door; she stood by the stove, by the simmering pots holding an already delayed meal. She had met the boy's surprise attack with a surprise tactic of her own, an eerie silence, a repressed calm.

With his hand on the limb of the pear tree, the boy watched the old man and the woman as they stood under the kitchen's ceiling light. His grandfather's lips moved; his mother's remained closed. If she should attack the old man, the boy resolved to fly to the rescue. The old man's lips continued to move as he stood by the white bowl trimmed with gold, as he talked above the mounded pears. The boy could read his grandfather's lips: Flyer and I will eat out tonight, the old man said as he took one pear, then another.

Once more, his mother did nothing. Her counter, the boy knew, would come later, and that would be as soon as her ally, the boy's father, returned.

The old man walked unmolested out into the night, walked with neither supplication nor wobble, walked across the dark yard. He continued walking until he stood in the circle of sand surrounding the tree.

—Flyer? he called.

From the darkness came a soft reply.

—Up here.

The old man arched his neck and looked skyward.

Season of Death

Autumn, the season of death, grips the land, where stripped crops dry and crackle in the sun. Spawned by the long drought of August and September, dust, the pagan saint of this sad carnival, settles over everything. In the town born when agriculture was king, remnants of harvest—peanut shells, shreds of tobacco leaves, cotton bolls, dingy chicken feathers—decay in the gutters beside the enduring styrofoam shells from the fast-food restaurants. Though the sun beats down hard on the scene, there is in it a hint of change, for it has a sharper, steadier focus. Grass withers and browns in the courthouse square. Trees in planters along the sidewalks drop yellow and brown leaves to scrape and scratch at the unyielding cement. Leaves slide along the sidewalk like an old man's shoes, like Artussa Joiner's as he walks away from his truck in the municipal parking lot, adjacent to the bank and across the street from the town's tallest building, the funeral home. Long ago the state's most elegant boarding house, it now offers short-term lodging for the dead. Designed as a house of life, grown to a house of death. Victorian, with gingerbread eaves and roof of shinning hammered metal, well-built and enduring.

They argue in Robert Davis's law offices. An incongruous pair, neither yielding. The young woman with pale blue eyes darting above plains of dark blue eye liner; the old man with watery eyes encircled by light red rims.

—An appointment, Lisa Ward says. Mr. Davis cannot see you without an appointment.

—Where can I buy a mint?

—*A Point Mint.*

—Point?

Lisa grabs a sheet of paper and writes emphatically. Seeing his teasing harden her face, Artussa grins. An old man can't get sympathy or understanding from the young; aggravating them is the only way to hold to pride.

—I never had to have an appointment to see the Colonel.

—The Colonel died before I was born; law offices aren't run like they used to be. Mr. Davis can see you Monday at—

—I'm dying. I need to see Little Colonel.

—You don't look that sick to me, Mr. Joiner.

—I'm not dying of sickness. That's not going to kill me. Decided long ago I wasn't going to die that way, paying a doctor while he hovers helpless as a hummingbird. Doctors got all this modern, colorful equipment and modern techniques, but they still stand over you and watch you die. And I'm not going to be like your grandmother either, pushing one of those metal walkers, while somebody says: You're doing good. There you go, you're doing just fine. Sliding to death on the arms of an aluminum walker. Those things aren't natural. I'll go cut me a sapling and whittle it down to a walking stick, but, by damn, that's it. I'll have something that was once a living thing or is a living thing holding me up, but not ore dug out of the earth, made into tubes, assembled at a factory, and sold at a damn hospital supply store. If something wants to keep me from falling, it's got to be capable of walking to me, or it's got to be something not far off my porch, something I can shape.

—Mr. Davis can see you Monday at ten.

—We've got nothing but low-grade ore in this soil, but seems like we think what's not made of metal is no good. Used to have fine, pine log tobacco barns. Now we cure the leaf in what looks like large metal coffins. I can't leave till I've seen the Little Colonel.

—Monday, Mr. Joiner. Lisa goes back to her keyboard. Her jaws working the chewing gum a little harder are the only acknowledgment of his presence. Artussa walks to the window and tugs at a large, shiny leaf, one of many similar leaves in a semicircle of potted plants. Plastic, the leaf doesn't yield. Artussa snorts, folds his arms, and drops into a chair.

The offices are located on the top floor of a three-story bank building. The top of the edifice is studded with gargoyles, mouths eternally opened as though devouring yet never sated, lifeless marble malice glinting in sunlight. Artussa doesn't notice that the sun's position casts the shadow of a widespread mouth across his head, the shadows of the teeth nipping at his long hair.

Lisa turns to glare at him and notices. She smiles as she turns back to her computer screen with letters bright green like the plastic leaves.

Artussa looks down through the sealed window at the street and at the cars endlessly going, knowing no season where machinery, in abeyance to cycles, slows, then lies dormant.

—How is your Grandma Ethel getting along?

Working the keyboard and checking the screen, Lisa ignores him.

Artussa looks briefly at the other occupants of the tiny waiting room: a skinny man with briefcase in lap and at a woman, who holds a sheet of yellow paper.

—What you folks here to see Little Colonel about?

—Mr. Joiner, please, Lisa pleads.

—I know that little one's Grandmother Ethel, Artussa tells the two strangers. Fact is, she's coming to see me today. She wouldn't

Generations

of been caught dead doing such silly mischief as that. Sitting on her butt all day and feeling a machine. Ethel could outrun my two brothers, could stack a load of watermelons better'n any man could. I lived with Ethel for two years after her childbearing days were done.

Lisa speaks softly but firmly into the metal intercom on her desk.

—That woman was something else. Never been a woman in this county who was as smart, as different, and as loving. She used to get up of a morning, walk naked out into the field and sit on a watermelon. And it be wet with dew and full of whatever coolness the night had brought. Got me to doing it, too. Both of us sitting out butt naked on swollen watermelons, feeling our *auras*. 'Can you feel yours, Tussa. Feel that energy that emanates from your body. You may think you own clothes, or watermelons, or these buildings, but, Tussa, dear, your naked self and your spirit are the only things you own. Nobody can own more.' She had a sweet voice, soft like a quail gathering its biddies.

—I may have been with Ethel yet if it hadn't been for that morning at the breakfast table when I kept pressing her on whether or not she was sure she couldn't get with child. She walked out and came back in with a jar. Stuck it beside the jar of watermelon rind preserves I was dipping out of. Hers was a great big jar. Had her ovaries in it.

—Mr. Joiner insists on seeing you *now*, Lisa says, her voice booming at the metal box on her desk.

—I couldn't stomach Ethel much after that. Every time I looked at any part of her I saw those ovaries. She might have them yet in the same jar. Maybe in Lisa's daddy's car trunk. Maybe on a shelf at the nursing home. You ought to get her to show them to you. That's your native land, child. All that come after you can trace their beginnings to that jar.

—Send him in, comes the delayed reply.

Robert Davis's neatly cut hair dips over his ears and conceals the wings of his wire-rimmed glasses. His face is tanned from weekends on the golf course. In no mood to see a garrulous, moneyless old man, he smiles as is his custom and extends his hand.

—Your granddaddy would be ashamed of you, Artussa says, leaving the waiting hand untouched. He knew you couldn't live without dirt, couldn't grow things. His floor was half-dirt and wasn't too good for a spray of tobacco juice. Air always found its way through these windows then. In the fall, if your nose was keen enough as mine was, you could smell the earth drying, and in the spring, the smoke from the new-cleared land. Now I sit and smell air-conditioning. I don't like to wait. I can't wait. And Lisa, Orvis and Belle's least girl, telling me I need an appointment.

—Makes it more efficient that way, Robert says. We can serve our clients better.

—Except for what's on me, there's no dirt in this office, but you traffic in it more than I ever did on a tractor. You even got the bathroom mopped and the toilet incubating blue water. I feel like a cucumber waiting to pickle.

Had Robert been following the old man closely, he would have agreed with the comparison. While not green, Artussa Joiner is rounded from top to bottom and has the color of the underside of a cucumber that has lain against the soil too long.

—I know what you want, Robert says. You talked to Truett's son, and let me tell you, he's right. Nobody's taken anything from you. It never was yours. I don't know what it was about your daddy, he was dead way before I was born, but my granddaddy tried to explain it to me one time. He told me that kind of thing seems to run in the Joiner family. Kind of like leapfrog is how he explained it. Like if your daddy told you he owned all that land, it would fire you with pride, make you go out in the morning spitting with spirit and work your ass off until you had twice the land he imagined he owned. Said your daddy always was a big talker, and Truett didn't half care what your daddy said. I can show you the papers verifying Tanner's ownership.

–I don't want to see your papers. All I wanted to do today was to tell you what I wanted to do with what I thought was my land after I'm gone.

–Only it isn't your land. So no worry there. Besides, when you leaving?

–There are always signs and portents, Artussa says. I've been seeing these two looking about what I thought was my place, checking my habits, seeing how feeble I am. They're coming tonight. Good night for them. Law enforcement will be tied up at the stadium and fair tonight. All them police and deputies checking out the young girls.

–Let me buy you a ticket to the game, Robert says. Sounds like that's the safest place you could be.

–Might be, but I'm not going. I'll be at home tonight, waiting on them. Maybe if I give them enough of a tussle, they'll go away respecting the old a little more.

–Old folks do have trouble getting respect, Robert says as he leads Artussa to the door.

–Only thing that bothers me about dying is that land. I got no children, but I think the feeling must be like a father dying when his children need his help most. I got a lot of things out there need me, and I wanted to leave the land to them as my legacy. Didn't want to ever see a 'For Sale' sign on it, or hunters or fishermen either. Didn't want it to be a museum. I just wanted to leave it be. Let the wildlife, even the little minnows have a haven.

—The Tanners won't sell it as long as you're alive, but you know this is boom country now. We got progress coming at us from all sides. People will be buying and selling land, using it in different ways. They always have. That's nothing to be upset about, Robert says while, with a deft move, repositioning Artussa in the waiting room. As Artussa looks back, Robert Davis's door is closed.

—Come back to see us, Lisa says.

—I haven't left yet, Artussa says, stopping in front of Lisa's desk and nodding to the others in the office. He begins talking of Lisa's great grandfather Sears's experiences in France during World War I, tells her about the French dancer wearing nothing but two acorns and some corn silk and how that dancer and Virgil Sears went to a hotel room with a white bed and white dresser and white chest of drawers all trimmed with gold, the dresser with a box of Havanna cigars and a red rose atop, and how the French dancer could say no English but *goodbye* and how Virgil could say no French but *au revoir* and how they spent a sweaty afternoon of farewells. Artussa is to the point of telling Lisa that some moments are so persistently intense that they attach themselves to you forever, is to the point of telling Lisa that Virgil was buried with the pasties and the silk g-string in his coat pocket when Robert, firmly though not in an overbearing way and in response to the frantic beepings from the machine, gathers Artussa in his arms, pushes him out of the office and leans into him to propel him down the narrow stairs.

—I forgot to tell Lisa that Virgil could lay out as straight a row with a mule as these boys do now with the big, fancy tractors, Artussa says, grasping Robert's hand in farewell.

Robert shakes his head as he climbs the stairs back to his office. Lisa is waiting at the top.

—I heard that, Lisa says. What does it matter to me whether or not Virgil Sears could plow a straight line?

Generations

—It matters because Artussa wants you to know that.

—I can't stand him, Lisa says.

—How can you say that about a man bravely going off to be killed?

—You don't believe that any more than I do. Nobody would want to touch him long enough to kill him. Even if it did happen I wouldn't consider much lost.

—How can you say that? Robert smiles. Seeing as how he and your granny were such good friends. That was, I hear, a scandal of most magnificent proportions.

—She wouldn't look at him now, Lisa says. I wouldn't let her.

Artussa used to say he lived way out in the country. Now he says in the country. The fast-food restaurants and other clutter of the town stretch so far along the highway; country is gone. His wooden house, clustered by chinaberry trees, seems chopped out of time, as unattached to today's world as a photograph of the past displayed for sale by an antique dealer.

A mile or so before the lane that leads to his house, Artussa stops his truck. This is his favorite spot this time of year, and he wonders if anyone else notices. What he loves is a bank of wildflowers, a last stand against the onslaught of winter. By the field of recently turned peanuts, whose vines have dried dark brown, a fencerow rush of weeds and wildflowers. Morning glories of lilac, brown-eyed Susans, and one flower he doesn't know by name but loves anyway. It is like a miniature bloom of a trumpet vine. The flower is dark red with five points like a star holding in its center a tiny white dot, like a narrow beam of light. The vine that supports the flower looks fragile yet is prolific, weaving its tiny self in and out of the morning glories and brown-eyed Susans, tying the arrangement together with green lace. It is nature's funeral offering to the dying land, a final song of color before winter's hush.

Artussa wades carefully into the flowers. His cracked fingers stroke the petals. He would not be a pirate of such beauty, so he picks one only of each type. Holding the bouquet of three flowers against his chest, he steps carefully from the fencerow and walks along the road behind his truck.

He is looking for the stain, the spot where an old dog fought death and lost. It is part of Artussa's shame that he didn't bury the dog, or at least drag him down into the ditch. Artussa, though, like all the others, veered to the left and let the dog lie.

Death had come in the night, a crushing metal death, a force with two bright, yellow eyes. The dog had turned his head to it much as he might have turned to watch a bird burst from cover, turned to stare death eye to eye. When life was over for the animal, death moved undiminished down the road. Life had ended for the dog, but not change. All who passed by, Artussa among them, saw the changes. The first they noticed was the dog, who had roamed their community for years, was now roamless, an unmoving mass on the shoulder of the road. The next change was the enlarging, death larger than life; the girth of the dead dog grew as gasses filled body cavities and stretched the skin so it seemed the bloated animal might rise from the road and float heavenward. When the weather turned cold, the swelling held for weeks. Then, suddenly it was gone. Perhaps the skin had given to inside pressure, or maybe a sliver of frozen rain had pierced the weakening shield of skin, maybe the beak of a buzzard testing to see if roadside picnic were ready. Whatever the cause, the swelling subsided, and the dog's body diminished. In early spring, the first white bone broke through the skein of worn skin; the remaining animal matter, a deflated pillow of skin and fur, molded itself to the roadside. Finally, in summer, even the bones were gone, borne off by some vandal of creatures. Only

Generations

those of the community, Artussa among them, knew why one patch of grass along the shoulder of the road was taller and greener than the rest.

That is what would happen, Artussa knew, if he were lucky enough to be left in grass. He would wax and wane as the dog had, as all who decompose do, and leave behind briefly a more succulent grass. If he were unlucky enough to be left in the creek, then his changes after death would pollute that which he loved. Frogs would hop to freedom, but minnows and the small fish he loved, trapped in his grave, would die. Should it happen that he meet death inside the house and be left to change on the pine floor, then, not now, not at first, but after all was said and done, one part of the floor would have a richer sheen.

Artussa stands above the stain on the pavement. He holds three flowers in his hand. The stems are cool; the flowers, holding some of the sun, are warmer. Artussa drops first the brown-eyed Susan, letting it fall like a plump bob to the center of the stain; then he releases the morning glory, watching it descend. This, he knows, is his funeral wreath for the dog and for himself. Days like this surprise him, days where the clarity of color and freshness of air make sweet his time among the living and cleanse him of any fear of death, though there is a flicker, something soul-like that craves life, something centered in the hurt of blood, like the white dot among the red of the star-shaped flower he holds to the last.

There are always signs and portents. One needn't be a psychic or medicine man to read them. Another sign for Artussa is Ethel Ward's visit. White-haired, listing to the left, her left arm barely functional, a string of drool lining the left side of her fallen mouth, this the Ethel who raised geese and gained the respect of Artussa, this the Ethel who could outrun his two brothers, who could load a truck with watermelons better than any man could, the woman who lived with him for two years after her childbearing days were done.

Artussa notices the walker. It looks foreign in the car; the walker's metal doesn't match the car's, the lines are askew. A calf wouldn't look any funnier riding in the back seat, Artussa says to himself.

–Mother just had to come out here today, Orvis Ward says, shaking hands with Artussa. If I'd been selling a car, don't think it would have made a bit of difference. Mother just had to ride out in the country today.

–I'm glad she's here, Artussa says, opening the door and patting Ethel's hand as Orvis puts the walker into position near the passenger door.

–Saw your daughter today, saw Lisa, Artussa says to Orvis.

–How was she?

–Might be coming down with something. Acted feverish there in Little Colonel's office. You know what this reminds me of? Artussa asks. Reminds me of the time Ethel's parents, they must of been close to eighty and couldn't hear no better than I can now, drove right up to where your car is, drove right up to the edge of the yard. Wanted to know if I was going to do right by Ethel, in light of the fact we had been living together for two years without benefit of clergy or legal niceties.

–'God Damn, Mr. Ward,' I said. They both thought I said "I am." They drove away smiling. Never did turn off the engine or get out of the car.

Orvis pulls his mother up from the car seat and centers her in the walker. She works her hands forward until she feels secure, then looks up at Artussa.

–Came out here to see if you are going to do right by me, Auratussa, she says and works her mouth to an injured smile, the

Generations

only kind she can give. Her words drag, but her voice is still soft and gentle. Her eyes sparkle.

–I am for sure going to do right by you. He leans over and kisses her. He doesn't mind the drool that sticks to his lips like sour milk.

–Mother tires easily, so we can't stay long. We'll visit a while on the porch. Let's go, Mother. There, just push it along. You got it. Doing fine. Doing fine. Mother can really get this thing going, can't she?

–Have to run to keep up with you two, Artussa says, waiting for them to catch up.

–Why don't you keep on running, Auratussa, Ethel says, and fix me some of your tea.

–Mother's not supposed to have caffeine.

–This I make gots lots of fiend, but no caf. That right, Ethel?

–You'll like it, Orvis, Ethel says.

–I'll fix the tea soon as we get you on the porch.

At the porch steps, Ethel holds on to the rail while Orvis moves the walker behind her. Artussa gets on her left side, and Orvis slips between his mother and the rail. The two men lift her up, step by step. She's a large woman, and each step feels to Artussa like he's lifting a gate post out of a deep hole.

The porch has rocking chairs and small tables. Board rails run between the posts. On top of the balustrades, Artussa has rusty tin cans filled with African violets. Under the porch, he keeps cuttings of azaleas and camellias. The moist ground under the water faucet is host to a bed of mint, nearing the end of its season.

Orvis and Ethel rock on the porch. Artussa goes under the porch. The rocking chairs are over his head, moving back and forth in rhythm. Artussa's fingers move back and forth as he kneels down among the mint, pinching off sprigs and adding them to the water, the tea bags, and slices of lemon, orange, and apple that are already in the gallon jar. The steady creak of the rockers dislodges dirt particles, some of which fall into the jar. What they don't know won't hurt them, Artussa thinks as he crawls back toward the yard.

–Are you keeping the cinnamon under the porch now? Ethel asks.

In addition to cinnamon, Artussa adds a little mustard and celery seed, and, while he's in the kitchen, he rinses out three glasses.

Back on the porch, he holds the jar before Ethel, who stirs slowly with her finger, creating a small water spout while yellow, orange, and red colors swirl beneath the surface. Ethel licks her stirring finger as Artussa takes the jar down the steps and out into the sunlight. He gives the jar a good shake, then puts it on the ground.

–Hurry back, Ethel urges. I want you to come sit by me and hold my good hand. Move over, Orvis.

They sit together for most of an hour this late afternoon. Ethel is the self-appointed sun watcher. When shadows creep over the jar, she points and one of the men moves the jar into the sunlight, usually Orvis because Ethel holds Artussa's hand tightly.

Orvis has to admit the tea is good and tells Artussa so several times on the long journey back to the car. Artussa fills the gaps between being thanked for the tea with thanking Orvis for bringing Ethel out to visit. In the sandy walkway, Artussa notes what strange tracks are left by shuffling feet and metal walker. Puts me in mind of those old dung rollers, he says under his breath. Pushing them a little roll of dung and it sticky and picking up bits of grass and sticks and sand as it moves. Those little bugs rear up to their larger burden and keep pushing. Push till they die.

Generations

Once mother and son are settled in the car, Orvis looks down the road while Artussa has his last words with Ethel: Stay, Ethel, he whispers. I'll undress you. We'll sit together naked where watermelons used to grow. See if between us we can splice an aura.

–You know I can't stay, but I'll be here in spirit. I'm often out here with you in spirit. Don't you drive off yet, Orvis. That tea was good, Auratussa, but I still need one of your kisses.

Artussa sticks his head inside the car. His long white hair drops across her face. As Artussa kisses Ethel, Orvis taps him gently on his shoulder. Good visiting with you, he says softly.

–Good to see you, too, Orvis, Artussa says, his face still close to Ethel's. Want you to do something for me, Orvis. There's a pretty bunch of wildflowers on the left about a mile up road. Pick some for your mother. There's a red star one she'll like. Red as watermelon heart.

Then they are gone. Ethel heading for her bed at Shady Acres, Orvis hoping to sell one car before closing.

–It's about this time of day I get most lonesome, he says, watching the trail of dust fan out behind Orvis's car and seeing on the horizon the dust rise as buses carrying the bands and teams drive toward the football stadium.

Now in the dry season, the creek sinks low in its channel. Rains of winter and early spring drive water over the banks; swirls of dark water charge past cypress and oak trees, swirl through piney woods, eat into white sand ridges. When the creek returns home, it brings back paper, rags, cans, and bottles, rafts of debris. By autumn it has dumped most of its garbage and moves sluggishly and clean. Leaves float upon its calm surface.

Artussa walks the dusty path from house to creek. He is naked. In his right arm he cradles a tin of saltine crackers, in his left a towel. His neck and arms are brown, but they no longer blaze as they did when he wore overalls and t-shirts while plowing the fields. The rest of his body is pale. Smooth flab jostles as he descends the path.

He hangs his towel on a limb, tosses three crackers out into the water. Sweeping leaves off the surface with his arm, Artussa settles in one of the few deep parts of the creek. Corpulent, he floats easily. His long hair spreads across the water then sinks slowly. He can feel the weight of his hair as it lowers. The small cracker flotilla bobs in the waves. Minnows attach themselves to the sides of crackers. Above, bats chase insects in the twilight.

Up the creek, as though sighting with the barrel of a long rifle, Artussa watches the dust hovering above the large lights of the stadium. The drums beat steady and loud. He feels his body responding to their incessant madness for he would sleep, but the drumbeat is pesky and picks, picks, picks, so that nothing is solid.

Artussa stirs his hands around in the creek and then stands. They're coming, he says. Water falls from his body in a rush like a sudden shower.

In fields around Artussa, pine trees are reclaiming land he once cultivated. The feed lot's farrowing pen, over which the sun descends like a flaming match, lies a pyre of twisted and rotten wood, a testament to the season. Artussa slaps his arms against his sides and rides out a shiver that moves the entire length of his body. It has been a long time since he's been grabbed by such a sensation. At first he doesn't know whether to curse or praise this feeling similar to the one he had sixty-five years ago when he waited his turn to box. Anxious then, he had known if things got too bad, too one-sided, one of his brothers would step into the ring and lead him back to the safety of his corner. Such cannot happen now, Artussa knows. There will be no intervener.